Sydnee,
merry Christmas. We
know you'll enjoy reading
this!!

Love,
mom & Dad
Christmas '81

SAM

Deseret Book Company
Salt Lake City, Utah
1981

SAM

JACK WEYLAND

© 1981 Deseret Book Company
All rights reserved
Printed in the United States of America
First printing March 1981
Second printing April 1981
Third printing November 1981
Library of Congress Cataloging in Publication Data

Weyland, Jack, 1940-
  Sam.

  Sequel to: Charly.
  I. Title.
PS3573.E99S2   813'.54   81-682
ISBN 0-87747-854-6

Chapter One

Y ou're going to try it again?" the boy asked as I walked with my son Adam across the park, carrying my latest model airplane.

"Just like last week," I said.

"Can you wait till I get my friends?" He stuffed an electronic calculator in his back pocket and ran toward a group of boys playing touch football.

I put the plane down, filled it with fuel, laid out the guidewires, and sat down on the ground with sixteen-month-old Adam, who was eating blades of grass.

"Adam, don't eat the lawn. If everyone ate the grass, what would become of our city park?"

"Some?" he offered, inviting me to share nature's bounty on a warm October day.

"If you eat grass, do you know what'll become of you?" I asked, ruffling his hair. "You'll grow big and strong like a Brahma bull. Is that what you want?"

"Some?" he offered again, leaning toward me to place it in my mouth.

I chewed and decided it wasn't half bad.

Far away, barely visible through the autumn leaves, I could see the bright reds and blues of the now-empty Ferris wheel where my wife and I began and ended our time together. I never went there anymore.

Turning back, I saw a cloud of boys approaching. They stopped just outside the radius of the plane's guidewires.

1

The first boy came to help me launch. In case he'd forgotten from the week before, I showed him how to start the engine, then returned to the control handle and nodded a go-ahead.

The plane was flying, drawing vanishing circles in the air and whining like an overgrown mosquito.

In a month of practice, I'd learned to keep the plane in level flight. But level flight was not what I wanted.

I banked the plane sharply upward in what was supposed to be a loop—then repeated the mistake of previous weeks. The plane went straight up, then straight down, and destroyed itself in a spectacular crash.

"All right!" the boys cheered and laughed—and left to return to their game.

The first boy lingered behind. "You do this every week, don't you."

"Yes, every week."

"Have you ever read anything about flying model planes?" he asked.

"No," I answered, sifting through the debris to find salvageable parts.

"They have books about it in the library," he said as kindly as he could.

"I'm sure they do."

"If you read 'em, you could learn and not wreck so many planes."

"Probably."

He nervously pursed his lips and looked at the wreckage. "It must take a lot of work to build a plane like this in a week."

"It does."

"When do you do it?"

"At night—I build them at night."

"But when do you sleep?"

"Between three and seven every morning."

He looked at me as if realizing for the first time that adults are mixed up too. "You can't sleep at night?"

I shook my head, at the same time dumping most of the shattered plane into a trash can. "That's why I build model planes, because I can't sleep at night."

2

"If you go to bed, maybe you'll be able to sleep."

"I can't go to bed," I said, realizing the conversation would have to end soon. How do I explain that a bed terrifies me, because when I lie down, I remember my wife Charly, who died five weeks before.

"Why do you spend so much time building something and then come out and wreck it?"

My voice had a bitter edge to it. "Nothing in life is permanent. Planes are no different."

He looked at me, trying to figure out what was wrong, and then gave up. "I'd better go now," he said, walking slowly away.

He caught up with one of his friends.

"Did you ask him?"

"Yeah, but he doesn't make any sense. You know what? I think he wants to wreck 'em."

On our way out of the park, we stopped and I pushed Adam in the swings.

Then a family came—a husband wearing Levis, a University of Utah sweatshirt and sneakers; a wife with long auburn hair in a ponytail that swung when she moved, in bluejeans and a long-sleeved shirt; a child, a boy older than Adam with red sneakers and bib overalls and a Sesame Street sweatshirt.

He stood protectively beside his son while she knelt in front of the swing. Each time the boy swung toward her, she reached for him, pretending she was trying to grab his foot.

"Gonna get your toes!" she teased, just missing with her outstretched hand, causing the boy to howl with delight. "Gonna get your toes!"

She repeated this several times, then paused while her boy calmed down a little. Brushing aside a few maverick strands of hair, she smiled at her husband as they shared the magic of the moment and the cascading laughter of their son.

I realized I'd been staring at them only when it registered that Adam, strapped in his baby swing, was complaining that he needed a push. I took one last look and returned to my duties.

3

"Nice day, isn't it," the husband said.

"Warm for October," I replied.

It was their family outing—they were happy—and I had to get away.

We stopped for ice cream on the way home. My boy gets plenty of ice cream from me, and too many toys from his grandparents—all that to make up for us burying his mother in a windswept grave in South Dakota.

It's fun to watch him eat a dish of ice cream. He does it with gusto. We've worked out an agreement. As long as I keep it moving fast enough, he'll let me use the spoon. But if things slow down, he takes things into his own hands, and the spoon isn't necessary.

What a handsome boy he is, even with ice cream dribbling down his chin. He has Charly's eyes—two dark olives staring at me.

Since returning to Salt Lake City I'd categorized each of his features into Hers and Mine, and had him marked off in my mind the way 4-H clubs do with cuts of meat from a beef carcass.

We went home and had lunch. My mother rightfully accused me of spoiling his appetite.

In the afternoon I helped my father clean out the garden, cutting down the cornstalks, pulling out the roots of the season's crops, clearing the ground. That's what we have to do when the harvest is over, when summer is gone, when winter descends. We have to pull out the old roots and think about next summer.

But what if there are no more summers? What if all that is left are cold gray winters?

A little later it was time for Adam's nap. I went in and lay down with him. I fell asleep but he didn't. He left me with only a stuffed beagle for company.

When I awoke I drove to the hobby shop and bought another model plane. Next week would also be long.

     *   *   *   *   *   *

The next day was Sunday. My father woke me up at seven as I lay curled up on an old sofa in the basement workroom where I build my planes. During the night I had made good progress on my newest model, meaning that I had been asleep for only three hours when he came to wake me. He had to shake me out of my dream. I always dreamed of Charly.

I got ready and we walked to priesthood meeting.

It is comforting to be with a group of priesthood holders and sense the strength in their lives. Priesthood is my favorite meeting now, maybe because nobody has his wife next to him there.

After church Bishop Andrews called me into his office and asked how I was doing and what I would like to do in the ward. I told him I wanted to spend as much time as possible with Adam, but would be willing to be a home teacher.

"Sam, one more thing. We have a single adult program in the ward. They have firesides and other activities. You should go to them."

I shook my head. "I don't think I'm ready for that yet."

"Well, maybe later then. And Sam—someday I hope you'll want to find yourself another wife."

I stared at the floor. "You never met my wife, did you?"

"No."

"Someone like her only comes along once every hundred years, so I have plenty of time before I need to start looking."

"Your boy needs a mother," he suggested gently.

"I don't mind if he has a mother. In fact I want him to have a mother—as long as I don't have to be related to her."

"Well, think about it," he said, standing up to shake my hand on the way out. "And if you ever need any help, just call me. I'm as near as the phone, and I want to help."

"Do you know anything about flying model airplanes?" I asked as I left.

After church Adam and I had lunch with Charly's parents. The nice thing about grandparents is they think everything their grandchild does is cute, even when he knocks over his milk twice, drops his plate of food on the floor, and smears butter in his hair.

After lunch the three of us went through a collection of Charly's pictures. We were working on a book of remembrance, deciding what to put in.

"And this is the good citizenship award she won in the sixth grade," her mother proudly explained, showing me the thirty-cent piece of blue ribbon she'd saved for all those years.

"It's nice, Mom. Let's put it in the book."

"Sam," she said, holding up a picture of a skinny nine year-old, "did I ever tell you about the time I baked a cake? She kept teasing me about licking off the frosting, sticking her tongue out. She got too near, and she did lick it. Of course I scolded her, but she said, 'But Mom, my tongue slipped.'"

"That sounds like her," I smiled.

The next picture was of a grown-up Charly, taken at a farewell party in New York before her family moved to Utah, just before I met her. She looked terrific.

"May I have the picture?" I asked.

"Of course—she was beautiful, wasn't she."

"Very." I put the picture in my wallet.

"You miss her, don't you."

"Very much," I said quietly.

"So do I, Sam, so do I."

*   *   *   *   *   *

Monday I went to work. It was my third week on the computer center staff at the University of Utah, doing routine programming and spending a few hours a day as a program consultant. That means that frustrated students throw their printouts on my desk and complain the computer doesn't work right. We slowly go through the error statements the computer so graciously kicks out and we clean it up.

Actually I find great comfort dealing with the cold logic of computer languages. Taped on my desk at work is a quotation from Albert Einstein: "One of the strongest desires that leads men to art and science is escape from everyday life with its painful crudity and hopeless dreariness, from the fetters of one's own ever-shifting desires. A finely tempered nature longs to escape from personal life into the world of objective perception and thought. . . ."

And that is where I escape every day from eight to five.

Chapter Two

I suppose it was obvious to everyone but me that sooner or later I would start dating. At first my mind formed vague images from old English novels in which I remained single and celibate as I devoted my life to raising my son as a memorial to my dead wife.

But I did start to date. The only problem was that my friends and relatives decided before I did that it was time to begin my life over again.

"It's just a fireside," my mother argued. "I promised her aunt you'd take her."

"I don't do firesides," I said, carefully gluing a strut for another plane.

"Her name is Mary Beth Rogers, and she's from Kansas. She's just here for a week. She's the niece of the Williamses across the street. She's a dental technician."

"Oh good," I smirked. "She'll teach me the right way to floss."

"She wants to go to the fireside."

"Mom, can you take her? I'm in the middle of a wing."

"Sam!" my mother warned in the voice she had used only when I robbed the cookie jar after school. "If you just keep coming down here night after night, wasting your time on these planes, I'm going to be very upset with you! Now I want you to take that girl to the fireside."

It wasn't too bad. The fireside talk was nice, the cookies homemade. Five minutes after it was over, we were in the car.

"Will you take me to the temple?" she asked.

"What?"

"I'd like to get some pictures before I go home tomorrow."

We drove to Temple Square, parked the car, and walked around.

"I want to get married in the temple," Mary Beth said as she gazed at its spires.

"That's nice—do you have a special person in mind?" I asked.

"No, do you?" she replied, looking at me very seriously.

"Do I what?" I asked.

"Do you have someone in mind?"

A long pause followed while I tried to sort out the conversation.

"For you?" I asked.

"No, for you."

"Oh, you mean, if I were to remarry, do I have someone in mind?"

"Yes, do you?"

At that point I started to sweat.

"No."

"Neither do I," she said. "That's one of the reasons I came to Utah."

"I see," I said blandly. "Well, good luck."

"As far as I'm concerned, that's the main reason for dating. Don't you agree?"

She was touching my elbow. I looked down to where she was touching, and then back to her. She smiled. I backed away.

Undaunted she continued. "What kind of a person are you looking for in a prospective wife?"

"I'm not looking."

"It's a commandment."

"To look?" I asked.

"No—marriage is a commandment."

"Well, as your aunt must've explained, I've kept the commandment once."

"But it's selfish of you not to get married again when there are so many worthy women."

"Oh, look!" I said, grasping for straws. "There's the Seagull Monument! Let's go see it."

I hurried to the monument, and she followed. "Mary Beth, you're going to love this story. The first year Mormons were in Utah, millions of crickets descended on the valley and began to eat the crops."

"I sew and cook," she said.

"The pioneers," I continued, talking faster, "faced certain disaster and so they prayed and soon the seagulls came and ate the crickets. Historians tell us they ate until their little seagull stomachs were full, then they vomited and went back for more."

"I'm good with children. I've been a Primary chorister."

"Mary Beth, it's interesting, don't you think, that the seagulls kept eating, vomiting, and eating again. What if they'd just had a little snack and flown away?"

"I know how to budget."

"Mary Beth, where would we be, I ask you, as a church and as a people, were it not for the gluttony of seagulls?"

She just looked miserably at me.

"Mary Beth, the members of the Church chipped in money for this monument to the seagulls. And look what that bird just did to it."

"What's wrong with me?"

She was about ready to cry. "There's nothing wrong with you."

She stood there. Any kind word from me would have helped. But I was no more comfort to her than the bronze seagull was.

"I'll take you home," I numbly told her.

We didn't talk again until I pulled in front of her aunt's house. I walked with her up the walk.

"I'll go back to Kansas tomorrow," she said dejectedly. "I guess I expected too much of one week here."

10

"I'm sorry I wasn't more help, but I'm empty. I'm on rock bottom and don't have anything to give. I'm sorry."

* * * * * *

The second date, a few weeks later, was also arranged. An old missionary companion, Dave Whittier, invited me down one Saturday to play some racquetball at BYU. We were finished by noon, then I bought him lunch in the Wilkinson Center. All through the meal, he kept talking about his cousin.

"An absolute knockout—get this, runner-up in the Miss Peach Blossom contest."

"Do you want any ice cream?" I asked.

Even through the ice cream he talked about her. I had managed to tune him out until I heard, "So I told her you'd pick her up at five for dinner and a movie. I was going to double with you, but I have to work tonight in the lab."

"I need to go home now. I got a lot of things lined up for today."

"Like what?"

"Model planes. There's one waiting for me now. Besides, my parents expect me for supper."

"No they don't. I called—they said it was okay. Anyway, they're having liver."

"Dave, thanks—I know you're just trying to help, but I can't just start over again. It's like asking me to go back to being seventeen and having to use Clearasil all over again."

He looked at me as though I was crazy. "You would stand up Miss Peach Blossom?"

"I thought you said she was just a runner-up."

"She was robbed—she should've had it. Look, just take her to dinner and a movie."

Eventually he wore me down and I agreed. After first taking a tour of his graduate research project, we went to his apartment, where I borrowed his razor and got cleaned up.

11

On my way out, shortly before five, he insisted I use his aftershave, called Tawny Leather. I was a little nervous and spilled half the bottle on my shirt.

"Don't worry," Dave reassured me, "it dries fast."

I showed up at her door smelling like a tannery.

She opened the door. She was all curls.

"I'm looking for, uh, Miss Peach Blossom—uh, I guess I don't know her name."

"I'm Elizabeth," she said softly with a nice smile. "Won't you come in?"

I stepped inside and wiped my sweating face. The aftershave was setting up a chemical reaction with my skin, turning my chest and stomach into leather.

On the wall was an original modern painting.

"Is the painting yours?" I asked.

"Yes, of course."

"I mean, did you paint it?"

"Yes."

"It's nice—a clown, isn't it?"

"No, a boat."

I helped her on with her coat. "A boat?" I stammered, looking at the daubs of color, trying to find a boat. "Oh sure, a boat. Well, we'd better be going."

By this time my forehead was drenched in sweat, and my stomach and chest were itching like crazy. In addition, I was about to be sick from the smell.

As we walked to the car, I took several quick breaths in rapid succession to clear out my lungs. She looked at me with just a hint of apprehension.

Once in the car, I rolled down the window to dilute the smell. My chest and stomach were on fire. I realized I wouldn't be able to stand it much longer.

"Would you mind if I took off my shirt?"

She continued to smile graciously, but edged toward the door just a little.

"Why?" she asked pleasantly.

"I spilled a bottle of aftershave on my stomach and I think it's reopening my belly button. I've got to do something."

"Oh, I see," she said, still smiling.

I rubbed my stomach. "I know what I'll do. I'll just go buy a new shirt. Okay?"

"You go ahead and do whatever you need to do."

A few minutes later, I rushed into a clothing store and barked out orders to an idle clerk. "I want a shirt, white, fifteen-and-a-half neck, thirty-three sleeve, and a glass of water. Bring them to the dressing room right away."

I hurried to the dressing room and took off my shirt. A few seconds later, he knocked on the door with the shirt and a glass of water. I thanked him and shut the door. Using my old shirt as a washcloth, I rinsed my stomach and chest and face, then dried myself with my coat. In a few minutes, I was finished and went out to pay for the shirt.

"Was everything fine?" the confused clerk asked.

"Just fine," I said.

I returned to Elizabeth, who was still smiling.

I asked her where she'd like to go to eat, and she gave me directions. I hadn't recognized the restaurant from the name, but once we were there I realized I had taken Charly there once during the first few months of our marriage when we had lived in Provo. I almost expected her to come running out and hop in the car with us. In other words, it was crowded.

I parked the car and stared at the restaurant.

"Is anything wrong?" she asked after a few minutes of watching me sit silently with my fingers locked tightly around the steering wheel.

"I can't go in there," I stammered. "You see, I had a wife and we lived in Provo for a while. There are too many memories here—she died."

"I know, Dave told me. Look, if you want to take me home, I'll understand."

I started the car. "This is no way to treat Miss Peach Blossom, is it? What a waste of a Saturday for you."

"Don't worry about that. I have tons of homework anyway."

"We could drive south," I suggested. "My wife and I never went south. Sometimes I just like to drive, don't you? I mean, if you happen to play the guitar, we could sing and drive."

"I play the piano and the trumpet."

"Okay, bring your trumpet along."

After picking up her trumpet at the apartment, we headed south.

It's amazing how much volume one trumpet can make in a car.

At Spanish Fork, we switched places and she drove, while I tried my hand, or rather lips, at the trumpet. It sounded like a moose with asthma.

Later we found a little cafe and had supper. There I had a better chance to look at Elizabeth. She was the ideal LDS coed—beautiful, thrifty, clean, and reverent. She'd make a good mother to Adam and she'd look good beside me in church. Someday perhaps I might even learn to love her.

Okay, why not? I'll marry her. It'll save me the hassle of dating a bunch of girls. Why not? Charly told me to go to Utah and find another wife. The only criteria she gave were to find someone who liked to cook and someone she could get along with.

Is it proper to propose on the first date? It would be nice to get it over with. I was in no condition for courtship anyway.

"Elizabeth, do you like to cook?"

"Sure."

"Wonderful. And I'll bet you like children too, don't you?"

"Of course."

"I was sure you would. Do you know how to change diapers?"

I'd gone too far. She looked at me strangely—the same way I'd looked at Mary Beth when she clung to my elbow and talked about marriage. I'd better not make the same mistake.

"Any particular reason for these questions?"

"Oh no," I said quickly.

A little past nine, I was standing with her at the door. "Elizabeth, can I see you again?"

"I guess so," she answered.

"How about every night next week?"

"Sam," she said, her forehead wrinkling for the first time that night, "I'm waiting for a missionary."

So what? I thought. I'll just dazzle her with the old charm and in a month we'll be engaged.

"Oh, that's nice." I smiled. "When does he come home?"

"Six weeks."

That's enough time, I schemed.

"I'll bet you're anxious to have him back after such a long time. Of course, he's grown so much on his mission, and you've changed too, haven't you? Still though, maybe you'll still have something in common, even after two long years."

"I thought you should know about Scott."

"I'm always interested in missionary work," I said enthusiastically.

She sighed with relief. "You'll think this is funny, but when you started asking me all those questions about children, I thought you were going to ask me to marry you."

"Really?" I laughed with her. "I just want us to be good friends. I guess it's obvious I need practice dating. Can we go out until Scott gets back?"

"I guess it'd be all right. For one thing, nobody's ever asked me to play my trumpet on a date. Are you sure you like it?"

"Oh, yes!" I said warmly. "Next time, though, could you bring a mute?"

My parents were up when I got home. Since I was whistling as I walked in, they turned off the TV and followed me into the kitchen.

"I'm going to get married again," I announced as I took some milk from the refrigerator.

"Oh?"

"Does she know that?" my father asked.

"Not yet—I have to proceed slowly. She's waiting for a missionary, so I have to let it sneak up on her, so she'll fall in love before she gets her guard up."

"Wouldn't that be wonderful?" my mother said. "What's she like?"

"She's very beautiful."

I found some cookies in the cookie jar, grabbed a handful, and sat down at the table.

"What else can you tell us about her?" my dad asked.

"She's a music major. That's good, isn't it? It'll save putting out money for piano lessons for Adam, if he wants them. She likes to cook. She loves children and knows how to change diapers."

"What's her name?" my dad asked.

"Elizabeth."

"Her last name?"

I dropped my cookie on the table. "I guess I don't know. I'll find out first thing tomorrow. I can ask Dave."

"How old is she?"

"I'm not sure, but she goes to the Y."

"You'll find all this out before you marry her, won't you?" my dad asked.

"Yes, don't rush into anything," Mom added. "You need time to adjust first."

"I'll adjust later—her missionary is getting back in six weeks. I want to have the wedding invitations out by then."

"You sound very confident," my father observed.

"My mission taught me about goal setting. Plan your work and work your plan. In two months we'll be married and Mom won't have to work so hard around here."

"I think this is much too soon for you," Dad said, "but I'll trust your judgment. At least there's one good thing about it."

"What's that?" I asked.

"If you do get married, you'll quit building those planes at night."

Chapter Three

They say Mexico City sits on top of layers of past civilizations. As soon as one culture died away, the next one built over it, with no thought of what was past and what was present and what was needed for the future. They should have separated what was dead from what was living. They should not have moved so fast in building on the warm ashes of the past.

"Hi, I'm Sam. I've come for Elizabeth."

A freckle-faced girl let me in and told me her name was Cathy. She motioned for me to sit down. There was a guy with her in the living room.

"This is Ben," Cathy said. "He just got back from his mission, and he's showing me some pictures. Liz will be a while so we'll let you look too. Did you go on a mission?"

"Yes."

"When did you get back?" Ben asked.

"Six years ago."

She whistled. "That long ago? So you must be a lot older than Liz."

"Six years older."

"You really don't look that old," she said.

"I take Geritol," I joked.

They don't like me just because I'm a little older, I thought. It isn't fair—I'm as immature as they are.

"What have you been doing since you got off your mission?" Ben asked.

"Computers and flying," I said, stretching the truth to make a good impression. "I fly every Saturday."

"Are you a student at the Y?"

"No, I work in Salt Lake."

"Where?" Cathy asked.

"The University of Utah."

There was a long pause and then she asked, "Don't they have any girls up there?"

"Elizabeth's cousin lined us up last week," I explained.

"You know she's waiting for a missionary, don't you?"

"Yes, she told me," I said brightly. "That's wonderful, isn't it?"

"Did she tell you her missionary is my brother?" she asked.

"Isn't that wonderful?" I repeated, my needle stuck.

"So naturally I'm wondering why you're here this weekend."

I looked at my watch and wondered if Elizabeth would ever come.

"Oh, look at this picture! Ben, I bet there's quite a story behind this picture. Tell us about it."

Cathy eyed me suspiciously as Ben gave a tract-by-tract account of what it was like to live in far-off Ohio.

Finally Elizabeth showed up, looking like Goldilocks with a trumpet case.

"I have a mute," she said first thing.

"What are you two going to do on your date?" Cathy asked as we started for the door.

"Make beautiful music together," I said, winking at Cathy.

*   *   *   *   *   *

"Isn't it amazing that we both have such an intense love for music?" I asked as we browsed in a music store.

"Do you play any musical instrument?" she asked.

"No, but I love music."

18

"What kind of music do you like?"

"I like all kinds of music!"

"Oh, look, here's a nice Brahms concerto," she said, picking up an album.

"Especially I like Brahms," I added. "Here, let me buy it for you."

"Oh, I couldn't let you do that."

"Nonsense, I want to make you happy," I said, picking up the album and carrying it with me as we continued.

Eventually we arrived at the instruction books for various instruments. While she looked at the books, I looked at her. She was the kind of a girl one could spend hours just watching, except it made her nervous, so I limited myself to looking when she wouldn't notice. It wasn't lust—more like visiting an ancient shrine dedicated to beauty. I could have easily knelt at her feet and given an offering of roses, but generally this is not an accepted activity for a date.

"Sam, if you love music so much. . ."

"I do! I love music!" I blurted mindlessly.

"Then you should learn to play something. What if I teach you a song on the piano?"

"You would do that?" I bubbled, thinking of all the practice time we'd have together, during which I could arrange for her to fall in love.

We looked through several piano books trying to find a song that would sound impressive but wouldn't be too much work.

"I've got it!"

The page was a forest of notes; it was called "Solfegietto" by C.P.E. Bach, whoever he was. Maybe the initials stand for certified public educator. Anyway, who cares?

"I couldn't ever play that," I said.

"Sure you can. Look—there's only one note playing at a time. I'll teach you."

We picked up the book and browsed some more, eventually passing the guitars and banjos.

"Banjos!" she said. "Sam, do you like banjo music?"

19

"Are you kidding?" I said, eagerly taking one from the shelf. "I love banjo music!"

"Me too."

"I think it's amazing how much we have in common," I said, plotting again.

She picked up another banjo and struck a chord. A big broad grin spread over her face. I struck a chord on my banjo.

"I've got a terrific idea," I said. "Why don't we each get a banjo and we'll take lessons together and learn to play 'Duelin' Banjos.'"

"We can't do that, Sam."

"Why not?"

"Look at the price tag."

"It's all right. I can afford it. This is going to be so much fun. We're going to be banjo pickers!"

The ecstatic salesman spent fifteen minutes teaching us a few chords and selling us an Earl Scruggs Self-Paced Banjo course with lesson manual and record. The bill came to two hundred seventy dollars. A small price to pay for a wife like Elizabeth, I thought, wondering if her missionary was having a nice day.

We went on campus to a music practice room and started on the piano first. Sitting next to her, smelling her perfume, and watching her curls sway as she moved her head made it difficult to concentrate.

"You're very beautiful," I said.

"Thanks," she answered lightly, tossing it off. "Now I'll play the first four notes here, and you play them here, one octave down."

"It looks impossible."

"It isn't. We just have to take it one note at a time."

"One note at a time," I repeated, looking at her. "That's what I'll keep telling myself."

My strategy was just that. She would fall in love with me if I just didn't spook her.

One week was gone and I was out nearly three hundred dollars.

Cathy became progressively more hostile each time I

came to take her roommate out. The next time I showed up she had a large picture of her brother on the coffee table and a calendar with the days crossed off. A large heart circled the day The Missionary was scheduled to return.

By the end of the third week, I had about played out any supposed common interests Elizabeth and I might have had. It was a gamble but I decided that she should meet Adam. Maybe he could win her over. I set up a date for Saturday.

That Thursday a lady who said she was a single adult representative in the ward phoned. She told me that the single adults were having a dance on Saturday and wanted to invite me, especially since I'd never yet been to any of their activities.

"I'm not sure I'll be able to attend, but thanks for inviting me."

"We have a band," she said enthusiastically.

"Well, I'll see how things go," which meant, no way.

Saturday afternoon I picked Elizabeth up in Provo, drove to Salt Lake City, and stopped by home to have her meet my parents and to get Adam.

The script for the evening was simple enough. We would go to a family restaurant, order a family meal, and get along like a happy family. Adam would be delightful. Afterwards, with tears in her eyes, she would tell me that this sweet boy needs a mother. I would drive to the temple grounds where we would walk. Gazing at the setting sun, I would close the deal by proposing. She would accept, and on the way home I would pull out some samples of wedding invitations and have her decide so we could get them in the mail to her missionary.

After that, I would need a little time to sort out my feelings—because I didn't love her. It would be like marrying the Statue of Liberty.

The whole thing had become an exercise in goal setting. Plan your courtship—courtship your plan.

Anyway it was a wonderful and touching script—one that Adam apparently didn't read.

The restaurant was crowded and the service was slow. Adam was starving and irritable because of a missed nap. At first he only whined for food and attention. Then he yelled—finally he screamed. Anxious not to create a scene, I went to the next table, where a nice retired couple were having supper, and I stole their crackers.

"Do you mind?" I asked above the roar of my son.

Apparently they didn't mind.

I ripped open the wrapper and gave him two crackers.

That quieted him for ten seconds, then he smashed the crackers with his pudgy little fists and tossed the mess on the floor. He screamed to get out of the high chair. I told him he couldn't get out, reasoning calmly in a loud voice.

Then he went into orbit, a classical tantrum, screaming and kicking.

I picked him up and carried him football style out to the car, tossed him in the back seat, locked the doors, and marched sullenly back inside.

I carefully cleaned up the cracker crumbs, wiped up the spilled water, and sat down. We were back to gracious living.

She looked at me as if I was a monster.

"You're just going to leave him locked up in the car like some animal?"

"He is some animal. You saw him. Yes, that's what I'm going to do."

"Well, I think that's terrible."

"He has to learn a lesson."

"It's very near being child abuse."

"I'm his father—I know what he needs."

"It could be a very traumatic experience for the child."

"The child?" I mimicked. "Elizabeth, this isn't some college discussion circle. This is real life! Real life is a very traumatic experience for all of us—or don't they teach you that in college?"

"Do you mind if I sit with him until you're through eating?"

22

"Yes I mind! What about your food?"

"I'm not hungry anymore—you eat it."

"If nobody's hungry," I exploded, "then why are we here? We might as well all sit in the car!"

Just then the waitress brought the food. I stood up, handed her a twenty-dollar bill, told her we couldn't stay, and asked her to give the food to the nice retired couple.

We drove silently home—silent because Adam had fallen asleep in her arms, and silent because Elizabeth and I weren't speaking.

We dropped Adam off with my parents and took off again. Even though I was starving, neither one of us dared bring up the subject of food again. I was at a loss to know what to do with the rest of the evening until I remembered the single adult dance.

When we entered, we were given name tags to fill out and were told they were going to have a little fireside before the dance. We found seats near the back of the room.

"Dorothy," the man conducting the meeting teased a lady, "have you and Albert anything to tell us tonight?"

The man next to Dorothy looked down at the floor with embarrassment. He was old and wore suspenders. "Not yet, Leroy, not yet."

"Well, you keep us posted now," the man conducting said.

Looking around, I realized these were old people.

"Let's get out of here," I whispered to her.

Try and find a decent movie sometime. We drove around for another forty-five minutes, ruling out the R-rated movies, finally settling on a PG, which must stand for Pretty Gross.

We didn't even stay to the end.

*   *   *   *   *   *

Less than two weeks to go and there had been no indication that Elizabeth was falling in love with me. I didn't

23

understand it. It was time to apply a little subtle salesmanship.

But first the agony of talking to Cathy at the apartment while Elizabeth kept me waiting.

"Elizabeth tells me you were married once and have a kid."

"That's right."

"You're looking for another wife, aren't you. That's why you keep coming to see Liz."

"I love music."

"No, that's not it. Well, I think you should stay up there in Salt Lake where you belong."

"That's an interesting opinion, Cathy. I appreciate your expressing it."

"Scott is getting back in ten days. What are you going to do when he's here?"

I smiled warmly. "I'll buy him a banjo too."

"Did you know he's an assistant to the mission president?" she asked.

"No, I didn't know that. That's nice."

"Were you ever an assistant to the mission president on your mission?"

"No, I wasn't."

"I didn't think so. Someday he'll probably be a stake president."

"Could be."

"I don't think you ever will."

"Probably not."

"It's not that hard to imagine him as a General Authority either."

"That's nice."

"You're jealous of him, aren't you."

"Cathy, it doesn't matter what our calling is. What matters is that we try to pattern our life after the Savior."

"I knew you were jealous."

"The purpose of the Church isn't to climb up some corporate ladder. If we can remember the Savior, then that will give us joy in whatever we do in the Church, no matter what our callings are."

24

She continued as if I hadn't said anything. "My oldest brother is a high priest, and he's on the high council, and he's even younger than you are. My parents say they're grooming him to be the next stake president. You're only an elder, aren't you?"

I decided to try one more time. "Cathy, a high priest isn't higher than an elder. They both hold the Melchizedek Priesthood."

"Someday you might make scoutmaster," she predicted, "or maybe ward clerk or Sunday School teacher, but you're just not stake president material. Sorry."

"It doesn't matter."

"Of course it matters, but you're just jealous. Sam, let me tell you something. There are just two kinds of people in the Church—those who are the leaders and those who are the followers. And you're definitely one of the followers."

"Cathy, let me tell you something. There are just two kinds of people in the Church—those who say there are just two kinds of people in the Church—and those who don't."

It took her several seconds to unravel that.

"I still say you'll never make high council."

Elizabeth and I had supper high atop the Wilkinson Center and then went to the music practice room to try "Duelin' Banjos." It sounded more like "Duelin' Mistakes."

Then we took a drive. By then I had installed a rather expensive car stereo. We listened to Brahms and drove by the homes overlooking the temple in Provo. I was trying to get her into a domestic mood.

"Ever dream of living in a house like that?" I asked.

"Sure—maybe in a hundred years," she smiled.

"Maybe sooner, Elizabeth."

"Oh?" she said, raising her eyebrows.

"I had insurance on my wife and we sold our home in South Dakota for a profit. I could buy a house in this neighborhood."

"Sam, is this a proposal?"

"Almost—it will be when you're ready for it."

Very kindly she said, "It's true what they say, isn't it?"

"What's that?"

"You try harder when you're number two."

My stomach tensed up and I felt an attack of failure coming on.

"You haven't seen Scott for two years. Time has a way of changing things. Maybe you won't feel the same about him when he returns."

"And that's what you're banking on?"

"I'm a decent guy—I'd make you happy. You'd have a nice dishwasher in a nice house, even a grand piano if you want."

"Anything personal in this, or are you just trying to furnish the house with a wife?" she smiled.

"Why don't you take me seriously?"

"Because you're not serious."

"I'm serious. I'll marry you tomorrow if you want."

"Oh, I think you're serious about marriage—but you don't love me."

"You're a nice person and I think you're beautiful."

"Thanks," she said lightly.

"I mean it—you're very beautiful."

"I said thanks."

"You treat it as if it weren't important."

"All right," she sighed. "I'm glad I'm beautiful."

"It's very important to me. I like to look at you. It's very inspiring."

"Inspiring?"

"It's like the first time I saw Hoover Dam."

She broke up. "Nobody's ever told me that before."

"It means a lot to me. I could watch you for hours."

"And what's my favorite color?" she asked.

"Blue," I guessed.

"Wrong. Which of my brothers is on a mission?"

"Ralph?"

"No, it's Larry. Have I ever had braces on my teeth?"

"I don't know."

"What classes am I taking this semester?"

"Let's see—"

"You don't know, do you. You're not interested in that. You just want me to be a centerpiece for your house and a mother for Adam. Then you'll fill in the rest by imagining I'm really your dead wife."

We drove silently to her apartment.

"Sam, I'm sorry for saying that about your wife. But I still feel as though you and I don't really know each other very well."

"I know Scott is coming back next week. Let me give you a little advice, okay?"

"Okay."

"Keep your options open."

She smiled. "Were you always this romantic?"

"I'm out of practice."

"Cathy's warned me about that—that a man who's been married, well, you know."

"What did you tell her?"

"That you were afraid of me. Sam, you haven't really gotten over losing your wife yet, have you."

*   *   *   *   *   *

Her missionary returned. The agreement was that I would give them a week to get reacquainted and then Elizabeth and I would meet in one of the practice rooms.

At the appointed time, I carried my banjo down the hall to our room.

"Well, you're here," I said.

She nodded politely. "Just like we agreed."

"Could we try 'Duelin' Banjos' just to warm up?" I asked. We did a pretty good job of it.

"Well, how did it go between you and Scott?"

"It went well."

"How well?" I asked, feeling miserable.

"It couldn't have been better."

I picked out a couple of chords to "Foggy Mountain Breakdown" and then forced myself to look at her. "You sound like someone who's just closed her options."

"I'm afraid so. I'm sorry it didn't turn out the way you wanted."

"I've learned a lot about music."

"I want to give back all the records and the banjo. It's not right for me to keep them."

"No, go ahead, keep them."

"Scott insisted I give everything back. The records are in that box."

"I don't suppose we'll be able to come here to play 'Duelin' Banjos' anymore, will we."

"No, not anymore."

"Well—could we try it one more time from the top?" I asked.

Chapter Four

I played it lightly enough for Elizabeth, but as the days passed I gradually came to the realization that I was trapped and might never escape.

I was a single adult.

You remember them, don't you? They are the ones who sit in the small pews along the sides of the chapel, the ones who leave quickly after sacrament meeting talks about the blessings of marriage and the family.

If I had a choice, I'd choose to remain forever a young married when Charly and I were poor students, eating a ton of pinto beans and week-old bread, going out together on her Avon route.

Or if I couldn't have that, I'd like to be a sophomore at BYU forever, a young adult, just off my mission, the man of the hour, optimistic and positive in my blue blazer, the choice of girls for Sunday afternoon supper invitations, the bright goal-setting eligible man on campus. That year everything seemed possible.

Now nothing seems possible.

And I don't have a choice.

The Church calls those over twenty-six and single, Special Interests. But my interests didn't used to be that special from anyone else's. I was interested in keeping my wife alive and healthy. I was interested that she not slip away from me, leaving me all alone with our precious little boy.

Nobody deliberately chooses to become a Special Interest. What sixteen-year-old girl would say that, when she grows up, she hopes she'll never get married and will work her whole life as a ploddingly faithful secretary in an office with only an eighth-inch layer of walnut on the walls, trudging home each night to an empty apartment and her African violets? Or that she wants to get married, have two children in quick succession, and suddenly find herself divorced—and all the while go to meetings to hear that marriage should last forever? Or that she will get married and that her husband and she will scrimp and save all their lives to raise children, send them on missions and through college, always with a dream that some day they'll travel—and then two months after retirement he'll catch a virus and never recover?

Nobody chooses to become a Special Interest. It's just something that happens. All of a sudden you find yourself the father of a two-year-old boy, and your wife is gone, and you're alone.

I am a Special Interest.

*   *   *   *   *   *

A week after Elizabeth and I had dueled our last banjo, the elders quorum president called and asked if I would home teach with Brother Porter.

He picked me up on a Tuesday evening near the end of February in his pickup with a new camper in the back. The back fender sported a sign that read, "When guns are outlawed, only outlaws will have guns."

"Nice camper," I said as I got in.

"Yeah—brand new. Guess how much I paid for it."

"Gee, I don't know."

"Go ahead," he grinned. "Just guess."

I shrugged my shoulders. "I don't know—maybe six hundred dollars."

"Six hundred dollars?" he snapped. "Are you kidding? It's worth at least seventeen hundred."

"Oh," I said.

An uncomfortable silence settled in.

"So guess how much I paid for it."

"I really don't know."

"Go ahead and guess."

"Okay—let's see, I'd say nine hundred."

His smile deflated. "Yeah," he said, looking very disappointed. "How'd you guess?"

"Just lucky."

"It's a steal, isn't it, at nine hundred?"

"Sure is," I said, playing his game.

"You bet," he said, running his fingers through his thinning hair. "I've already been offered fourteen hundred for it, but I won't take it. No sir."

He went into some detail on how he happened to make such a good deal, and I found myself in the role of admirer, needing only to say occasionally, "Is that right?" and "Boy, you really did well, didn't you!"

Finally at a stop light I asked, "Who are we visiting tonight?"

"Oh, don't worry. We've got a good home teaching beat—all active people, very few problems. They all go to church, and none of them smoke or drink. Usually I can wrap the whole thing up in a night. Say, you ever been to the Uintahs?"

The first stop was a gray four-story apartment house built in the forties. We knocked on 312. The door was answered by a round-faced girl in her late twenties. Her name was Shirley Benson, and she worked as a seamstress in a lingerie factory. She invited us in, and Brother Porter introduced us.

She smiled. "I hope you like dessert, because I treat my home teachers every time they come. Isn't that right, Brother Porter?"

"You bet! I'll never forget that coconut cream pie last month."

She asked if I was married and I explained my situation, something I had learned to do quickly in matter-of-fact tones. I cried only at night now.

We had cake and ice cream.

"Sam, have a little more."

"No, thanks—it was delicious though."

"Oh, go ahead," she encouraged. "It's not fattening."

Brother Porter had more.

A minute later, Brother Porter took one last drink of water, sat back in his chair, sucked air between his front teeth to remove any food particles there, and started his lesson.

"I have this little book with some real nice stories and I was reading one just before we came over. It's about these two frogs. It seems they both got trapped in a farmer's milk bucket. Well, they tried and they tried, but they just couldn't get out. After a while one of the frogs got discouraged and just gave up, and he drowned. But the second frog, he wouldn't give up, and just kept swimming. And you know what? After a while, all that swimming churned the cream into butter, and that old frog just walked out of the bucket. That's a great lesson to all of us, isn't it? No matter how bad things get we just have to keep swimming and never give up."

"That's so true, isn't it?" Shirley said, picking up the plates. "We do have to keep swimming, don't we. Thanks, that was a great lesson."

"The lessons are the easy part," Brother Porter grinned. "I'll keep the lessons coming if you keep the treats coming."

We had a prayer and left.

"Well, that didn't take too long, did it." Brother Porter observed as we got back in his pickup.

"Is she trying to do anything about her weight problem?" I asked.

"I don't know—she probably likes being fat. Besides, it's none of my business."

Our second visit was with Joan Anderson, a divorced woman in her early thirties with a two-year-old named Melissa. Three months ago she had been living in Denver with her husband, but one day he left her for another woman. Joan had moved to Salt Lake City so her mother could babysit for her during the day while she worked as a waitress in a pancake restaurant.

She opened the door, saw us, and gasped. "Oh—I forgot you were coming. Gee, everything's a mess."

"We don't mind," Brother Porter assured her. "Besides, we won't be long."

She let us in. She was right about the mess. She'd been sorting clothes before going to her mother's to do the laundry, and she had a pile of whites and a pile of coloreds on the living room floor. Toys were strewn around the clothes.

Brother Porter introduced me to Joan and her daughter Melissa. Soon after sitting down on the worn couch, I discovered I'd sat on an old piece of toast with peanut butter on it.

A little light talk about the weather and then we went on to the lesson.

"I have this lesson about these two frogs. You see, these two frogs got trapped in a bucket of cream."

Melissa appeared from the bathroom with no clothes on.

"Melissa, you get your clothes on," her mother warned.

"No!" Melissa insisted in her best terrible-two-year-old voice.

"Excuse me," Joan said, heading for her daughter.

The TV was still on. As she left the room, we automatically turned our attention to the program. It was an adult love story—siphoned from the flow of real sewers.

"I can't believe they show that on TV, can you?" Brother Porter asked as we watched.

"No, I can't," I agreed.

We heard Joan slam a door, lock it, and then she returned.

"Sometimes I have to lock her in her room," she said, looking very tired. "Excuse me for the interruption. Go ahead with your lesson."

"Well, there were these two frogs, you see, and it turns out they got caught in this bucket of cream."

"LET ME OUT!"

"I'm sorry," Joan said, distracted by her daughter's yelling and banging on the door, "but what were you saying about a frog?"

"There were these two frogs . . ."

"I WANT OUT!"

". . . and they got trapped . . ."

"LET ME OUT!"

". . . in a bucket of cream . . ."

"MOMMY!"

"Excuse me," Joan said, marching back to the bedroom.

Again we turned our attention to the TV, rationalizing that we wanted to find out how rotten things have become.

One scene was particularly bad, especially for me because I didn't have a wife to go home to. I'd probably be up late working on a model plane again.

Then it proceeded from bad to rotten.

"I wonder if she'd mind if we turned it off," I finally said.

"What?" Brother Porter asked.

"I shouldn't be watching that," I said.

"No—it's terrible, isn't it. I wonder who watches that stuff."

"I'm going to turn it off now," I warned.

"Right now?" he asked.

I turned it off.

"Terrible," he said. "It's a wonder they get away with showing that. You know, people could avoid the mistakes that couple was making if they'd just get themselves a good hobby—like fishing or hunting."

"Or model planes," I agreed.

"You ever notice on TV, they never have a guy involved with another woman if he's a trout fisherman?"

Joan returned with Melissa dressed in pajamas with the zipper pinned shut.

"Now I'm ready for your lesson."

"I hope you don't mind, but I turned off your TV."

"Was it on? I never even notice anymore—it's just nice to have adult voices in the room."

Brother Porter cleared his voice and talked down to Melissa. "Now Melissa, you listen real carefully because I'm going to tell you a nice story. It's all about these two frogs, and one day they got caught in a big bucket of cream . . ."

Melissa drifted out of the room.

Before Brother Porter could get the frog out of the bucket again, Melissa appeared from the kitchen, covered from head to toe with flour, looking like a grinning ghost, tracking white as she walked.

"MELISSA!" Joan yelled, chasing her, spanking her hard, sending up little clouds of flour with each whack. A second later, a white screaming Melissa was hauled into her room and locked in again.

"MOMMY, LET ME OUT!"

Joan looked as though she might cry, but she didn't. She just collapsed into her chair, held her head, and asked us to finish so she could get the mess cleaned up.

"Oh, sure," Brother Porter assured her, and quickly polished off the frog story.

"Thank you," she said numbly, after being told to keep swimming.

"We'll help you clean up," I said.

"You don't have to."

"We're world authorities about cleaning up flour from kitchen floors."

"Of course we would like to stay and help," Brother Porter backpedaled, "but we have other appointments tonight."

"Call and tell them we'll be a little late," I suggested.

"One is an old lady who goes to bed at eight-thirty."

"Then we'll visit her tomorrow night."

"I go bowling tomorrow night."

"We'll go right after work then."

By then I was already sweeping, so he decided to help.

Sometimes a frog can't escape the bucket all by itself.

＊　　　＊　　　＊　　　＊　　　＊　　　＊

The next day about five-thirty Brother Porter picked me up again.

"Well, two more visits and we'll have it wrapped up for another month," he said. "The first one is Sister Hilton. She's a retired schoolteacher—lost her husband a couple of years ago. She's doing all right now—completely active in the Church, so we don't have to worry much about her. She even does genealogy. I usually just visit with her a couple of minutes. Completely active—okay?" he stressed again so I'd know she was problem-free.

"Okay," I said.

She lived in a small house. There was a broken board on one of the steps of her porch.

"Careful of the step," Brother Porter warned me well in advance.

"We can't stay long," Brother Porter cautioned as we sat down after the introductions, "but we just wanted to drop by and see if everything is all right."

"Just fine," she said.

"You're healthy and strong?"

"Fit as a fiddle."

"Got enough food?"

"Certainly," she said, sounding a little insulted.

"How about family home evening?"

"Well, there's just me now . . ."

"Well, we'll count you as having it. Our lesson today is about these two frogs . . ."

I was sitting near a window. There was a continual stream of cold air pouring into the room on that cold winter day. I turned around to look. She didn't have her storm windows on, and there were large cracks that needed caulking. I wondered how much her heating bill was.

The room was filled with the usual knickknacks given long ago and never discarded. It was what you'd expect from a retired teacher, with the exception of a giant pot-

36

ted palm near the door to the kitchen. It was seven feet tall and extended well into the room, something you might find in a musty second-rate hotel, not in her tiny house.

". . . so it just goes to show you—when things get rough, we have to keep swimming. And that's our lesson for tonight."

"Thank you, it was nice. Will you stay for a piece of cake?"

"Gosh, we'd like to, but we have another appointment in a few minutes."

"Sister Hilton," I said, "that's an interesting potted palm."

"Oh, that. I hate it, don't you?"

"Well, it is a little large for the room."

"Would you like to hear how I got it?"

Brother Porter checked his watch. "Some other time, okay? We really do need to run now."

"It's not a long story," she said.

"I'd like to hear it," I assured her.

"My husband and I taught school for forty years. Even after he died, I stayed in the same school. Then it came time for me to retire. During the last school assembly, a student was giving a talk and mentioned I was retiring. I saw a look of shock pass over the principal's face and knew he'd forgotten to get me anything for my retirement."

Brother Porter jangled his keys.

"Of course, I didn't want much, but it was as clear as day that he'd forgotten. After the regular program, he got up and gave a little talk about my retirement. While he talked, his eyes fell on the large potted palm they kept on the stage. He walked over to it, picked it up, called me from the audience, and presented it to me."

She stood by the palm. It was much taller than she was, and seemed almost to engulf her.

"And that's the story of my palm tree." Her voice had a bitter edge to it. "I hate it, you know."

"Why?" I asked.

"Forty years' teaching, and that's what I have to show for it."

"Well," Brother Porter cheerily announced, "that's sure an interesting story!" He stood up, ready to leave.

"But you keep it," I said.

"Yes."

"Why, if you hate it so much."

"Because we have a common bond, don't you see? We're both discarded and useless now. So we stick together. It wasn't the palm's fault. Yes, we hate each other, but we're all we have now."

Brother Porter had his jacket on and his hand on the door.

"What do you do with your time now?" I asked.

"Not much. I do genealogy for my ancestors. I think they appreciate it."

"I'm sure they do."

"Although they aren't much for conversation."

Brother Porter left.

"Sister Hilton, I'd better go. One thing, though—I noticed it's cold around that window. Do you have storm windows?"

"I guess so—my husband always took care of that. I haven't felt like going down in his workroom in the basement and looking around—to see his tools just the way he left them."

"Let me come over Saturday morning and put the storm windows on for you. All right?"

She looked at me strangely. "Do you really mean it?"

"Of course I do."

"I'd appreciate that very much."

I hurried to the pickup, and Brother Porter headed quickly for our last stop.

Paul Wilson lived in his aunt's two-story house and looked after it while she was in Arizona for the winter. He was a physics student at the University of Utah.

When he opened the door, he was carrying a large metal serving spoon in one hand. He was tall and skinny, wore thick glasses, and had an absent stare about him, as if never completely sure where he was.

38

"Yes?" he asked at the door.

"Don't you remember me?" Brother Porter asked. "We're your home teachers."

"Oh," Paul said, letting us in.

Even as we sat down, he continued to look at his reflection in the spoon, first from one side and then the other.

"Well, Paul, how's it going?" Brother Porter asked.

Paul looked up at us with a blank stare.

Brother Porter glanced over at me and shrugged his shoulders.

"Say, that's a big spoon you got there! About to have a big dish of ice cream?" Brother Porter chuckled at his little joke.

"No."

"I see—just looking at the spoon, huh?"

"When I look at it this way, my image is right side up, but when I turn the spoon over, my image is upside down. Want to see?"

He handed us the spoon and we both tried it.

"Say, that's right!" Brother Porter exclaimed.

"In one case," Paul continued, "the image is virtual and erect, while in the other case, it's real and inverted."

"Heck of a deal!" Brother Porter said, checking his watch. "Well, I guess we'd better go to the lesson. I think you'll really enjoy this. You see, there were these two frogs . . ."

Three minutes later, we stood up to leave. "If there's anything we can do, don't hesitate to call us," Brother Porter said, shaking Paul's hand.

Paul was confused. "What?"

"You know, if you have problems, we can help," Brother Porter said, putting on his coat.

"I have problems," Paul said simply.

That caught Brother Porter off-guard, and he quickly backpedaled. "Well, of course, everybody's got problems."

I wasn't going to let Brother Porter just ignore Paul and his problems. If Paul needed our help, then we would help.

"Paul," I asked sympathetically, "would you care to talk about your problems?"

Brother Porter checked his watch again. "I don't know if we have time to go into Paul's problems right now. Paul, how about next month when we come?"

"We're his home teachers! Why do you make these visits anyway?"

That caught Brother Porter by surprise. He glared at me.

"Go ahead, Paul, tell us about your problems," I said, my voice dripping with compassion.

Paul put his big spoon down and looked at me. "I'm not sure you'd be interested in my problems."

"Of course we're interested," I said, glancing at Brother Porter. "And we'll help you, even if we have to stay till midnight."

Brother Porter looked at his watch and mumbled something.

"Now go ahead," I continued. "Sit down, if that'll make you more comfortable. Tell us about your problems."

Paul sat down and looked at me with a curious expression. "Okay—if you're sure you're interested."

"Trust us, Paul."

Paul looked down at the floor and began. "I'm supposed to derive with the help of the method of saddle point integration a formula for the partition function of an ideal gas composed of integral spin Bose particles."

We both stared at Paul with our mouths wide open. There was a moment of silence.

"I didn't think you'd be interested in my problems," Paul said.

"Oh, that kind of problem! I thought it might be another kind of problem. Paul, is there any other kind of problem in life you'd like to talk about?"

"No, not in life."

"Good man!" Brother Porter exclaimed, slapping Paul on his back. "Well, just remember the story about the frogs! It gives us a lot to think about, doesn't it?"

"Yes—I've been thinking about it," Paul said.

"See there?" Brother Porter smiled triumphantly at me.

"I wonder why the farmer didn't take better care of his cream."

"We gotta run now!" Brother Porter announced, escaping to his pickup.

On the way home, I told Brother Porter about offering to install Sister Hilton's storm windows.

"Fine, go ahead."

"Can you help?"

"No, I'm going to get some more wood for our fireplace."

A few minutes later, he parked his truck in our driveway. "Five years of one hundred percent home teaching," he said proudly.

"It's good you visit them every month."

"I guess so, but you know what? You seem to care about them a lot more than I do."

"Maybe because I'm single like they are."

"If you want, I'll talk to the elders quorum president about having you work with them. Maybe you can help them, Sam."

I shrugged my shoulders. "I don't know—I'm not sure I can even help myself."

"Let me give you a little advice," he said.

"Okay."

"Just keep swimming and before you know it that old cream's going to turn to butter."

Chapter Five

Time passes. Whatever else you can say about life, at least you're guaranteed that.

Some see time marching grandly onward like a military parade. Others view it as flowing, a river emptying into an endless sea.

But to me time halts and limps and then lurches forward, like a wounded sailor in a foreign port trying to make it to his ship before it sails at dawn.

Six months had passed since my wife's death; the original white-hot ache had decayed to a bleakness of routine and duty and responsibility.

The turning point occurred in March when the bishop called me to be one of the single adult representatives in the ward. We met once a month with our ward committee and also once a month with the stake committee.

At my first stake committee meeting, I met Jon Stevens. We were both about the same age. He had never married.

He told me he was building a boat from a kit and said if I'd help him with it, he would let me use it anytime I wanted. Once a week after that, I bundled Adam up and we went to Jon's garage and worked.

He was sort of a cross between the Marlboro man (with no cigarettes) and a young Archie Bunker. Sometime after he turned eighteen he must have sat down and taken a stand on every possible political issue. We spent hours arguing politics as we fitted and glued and sanded and painted.

Another source of interest in my life came from home teaching. Two weeks after going with Brother Porter, I was assigned his route.

My home teaching companion was a senior in high school who was involved in sports. I was happy for his success but sometimes found it difficult to arrange a time to go out with him home teaching. Sometimes I took Jon with me even though we weren't in the same ward.

One day after church, Shirley told me she had joined a computer pen-pal club and had been writing a man who lived in Pennsylvania. She had told him about the Church and he was taking the missionary lessons.

Three weeks later she told me he had been baptized.

And then, a few days after that, she asked me to come over that night, because she had something important to talk to me about.

Since my regular home teaching companion was out of town, I asked Jon to go with me. When we arrived, she told us her pen pal wanted to meet her, and maybe even marry her, and that he was coming in five weeks.

"That's wonderful," I said.

She burst into tears. I asked her what was wrong.

"This!" she said, handing me a picture of her taken forty pounds earlier. "I sent him this. He thinks I look like that."

"Oh, well," I stammered, "looks aren't everything. Nobody can top your bright happy smile."

"I'd still have the same smile if I were thin," she cried.

"Good grief, lady!" Jon barked, unable to cope with crying women. "If you don't like being fat, go on a diet!"

"I can't! It won't work! I've tried it before."

"We'll help you this time," I said. "Won't we, Jon?"

"Hey, you help her. I'm not her home teacher."

"Jon, won't you help her any?"

"Oh, all right!" he barked, turning to Shirley. "Look,

if you don't want to be fat, then don't eat so much! Quit stuffing your face!"

Then he turned back to me. "There, I helped."

"What he means," I said, trying to smooth things over, "is that if you carefully plan what you eat, you're sure to lose weight."

"And get off your duff and get a little exercise too!" Jon added.

"Perhaps," I translated, "a little exercise would be helpful too. I think that's what Jon is trying to say, isn't it, Jon?"

"I got no respect for somebody who gorges food," Jon muttered.

"Fred plans on coming from Pennsylvania in a month," she said. "Can I look like I did in this picture by then?"

Jon grabbed the picture and compared it with Shirley. "You've really let yourself go, haven't you. I wouldn't be caught dead looking the way you do. Your arms—look at that flab—they make me sick."

She cried for a while and then stopped and smiled. "Where did you find him—in an old Gestapo movie? But you know what? I like him. I think he's just what I need now."

We wrote down some rules for eating and then talked about exercise at the Deseret Gym. "Jon, will you work out with us too?"

"I'll work out with you," he grumbled, "but don't expect any leniency. When I work out, I work out—none of these namby-pamby exercises. I'll run you both into the ground."

A few days later I got Jon onto a racquetball court. I didn't try for the immediate point, but instead ran him after the ball from the front to the back court, while I stayed in the middle and watched him sweat. By the end of the second game, his sweatshirt was dripping wet and he was uncharacteristically quiet.

"Thanks for the game, Jon," I said, smiling. "How about another one?"

44

He was too busy breathing to answer me.

Shirley was my next opponent. When she entered the court, I had to force back laughter. She was wearing layer after layer of gray sweat shirts and pants, and she looked like a dreary version of the Pillsbury Doughboy.

But she was a game girl and never gave up.

After racquetball we exercised, working on our individual tummies. And after that, there was swimming.

And then supper—two fillets of fish and a tossed salad.

It was hard on her at first, and she phoned every night about nine-thirty so I could talk her out of a bedtime snack. When she called, I calmly reasoned with her that the body can only store the food eaten at night because there is very little need for it during sleep.

After a few days of my calm reasoning, she quit calling me and started to call Jon because he was more effective in helping her curb her appetite. "You think I want a tub of lard for a friend?" he'd say in his usual subtle, well-thought-out manner.

"Thanks, Jon. I needed that," she'd say, and hang up and go without food.

Each time she got a letter from Fred in Pennsylvania, she would phone and read part of it to me. She was very excited about his visit, and that she was losing weight.

Finally the week arrived for his visit. The day before, Jon and I bought her a new dress. We knew her dress size. In fact, we knew all her measurements, because we'd plotted her progress. I'd made up a little computer program that gave her a week-by-week printout of what she'd accomplished since the beginning of the diet. Somehow, having it done by a computer made it more official to her.

When we gave her the dress, she started to cry.

"Hey, none of that!" Jon growled, but I could tell he was just a little emotional himself.

"You two have been so good to me," she sniffled.

"It's been okay for me too," Jon admitted.

"I'm so excited about tomorrow," she bubbled a little

later as she modeled the new dress. "His bus gets in at four o'clock, and then we're going out for supper."

"Skip the dessert!" Jon warned.

The next evening as I washed diapers and helped my mother around the house, trying to ease her burden of caring for Adam every day, I wondered how Shirley was doing.

I didn't have to wonder very long, because at eleven o'clock she phoned me and, in tears, asked me to come over. I phoned Jon and he grumbled a little, but then said he would pick me up in five minutes. Jon always picks you up—you never pick Jon up.

At first she just cried.

"Something went wrong tonight, I bet," I said.

More tears. She had her head buried in a couch pillow.

"Let's see—did he show up?"

"Yooaah!"

"Is that a yes?"

She nodded her head.

"So he showed up. Well then, let's see, he doesn't want to get married. Is that right?"

"Nooaah!"

"He does want to get married? Then what's wrong?"

"Nano me!" she sobbed in the pillow.

"Shirley, I can't understand you. What does 'nano me' mean?"

"Not to me!" she called out, lifting her head up for a second, and then burying it back into the pillow.

She cried, and I thought, and Jon, who had to be at work at five the next morning, sat and yawned.

"Not to you—he wants to get married but not to you. Who to, then?"

After a few minutes she sat up and talked. "He got off the bus, shook hands with me, and introduced me to a tall blonde girl. She'd gotten on in Chicago, and they'd talked, and her parents have quarter horses on a ranch, and he loves horses, and she invited him to stay with her folks in Heber. Then they collected their bags and left.

46

She took my convert! It's not fair! If things like that can happen on a bus, then Greyhound ought to warn people about it. I should've told him to fly!"

She started to cry, stopped, and said very deliberately, "Sam, I want you to get me the bag of marshmallows in the kitchen."

In a minute I was back, and she put a marshmallow in her mouth.

"How can a blonde get a tan in Chicago? And what's so neat about quarter horses anyway?"

In a minute, she had another marshmallow.

"They're going to get married, you know. That's what's going to happen. Do you know what I hope? I hope all his children are as blonde as their mother, and someday I hope they all go to the beach and fall asleep in the sun and get terrible sunburns!"

She cried some more and continued eating.

"What's all this gotten me?" she complained. "Before I was a fat miserable girl, now I'm a skinny miserable girl." A minute later she said she wanted some hot chocolate to go with what was left of the marshmallows. We went into the kitchen to make it. Just before the water boiled, she turned to me and said, "It's never going to happen to me, is it. I'm never going to get married in the temple and have a family."

"It could still happen, Shirley."

"Yeah, but you don't believe it will, do you?"

"Miracles still happen."

She shot a withering glance at me.

"Not that it'd require a miracle," I backpedaled.

We poured our cups of hot chocolate and sat down. Jon was snoring in the living room.

She stared at the melting marshmallow in her cup and shook her head. "It's so hard, Sam, you know that?"

"The marshmallow?"

"No—being twenty-eight and single. It's a lot harder than being a teenager. Why do we worry so much about teenagers anyway? They grow up and become just like us."

"That's why we worry. We hope they won't be like us."

"When you're seventeen and nobody is taking you out," she continued, "you dream about a missionary who'll come back and marry you. Well, that's been my dream for twelve years, and tonight the bubble burst. I finally realized it's never going to happen."

I took a drink of hot chocolate and burned my tongue.

"I guess I should've realized it when I read that one of the boys from my high school class was called to be a mission president. And I'm still waiting for a missionary to come back. But tonight—tonight made it crystal clear."

I guess I agreed with her. It might never happen in her life.

"So what's left for me?" she asked. "Sitting in the back row of the chapel, hating the young mothers ahead of me with their noisy kids and Cheerios and diaper bags and husbands. It's not fair!"

"I know—it's not fair."

"So what good is my well-protected virtue?"

I choked on my hot chocolate. "What?"

"If I can't have an eternity of love, how about one night of it?"

I stood up and suggested we go into the living room with Jon.

"Not with you, Sam."

"Oh," I said, relieved.

"Unless you want to," she said.

"Well no, actually. You see, I've always valued my membership in the Church, and I'd hate to get excommunicated, and besides that . . ."

"Relax," she smiled. "Do you know where I went after Fred left me? I didn't want to go home, so I decided to go to a movie. And I walked around from one theater to another trying to decide, and even the posters embarrassed me. Finally I found a Disney movie and went in and watched it, ate popcorn, and cried. But those other posters got me thinking—maybe I've been missing something in my life."

"You can't do that."

"Why not? Every movie in this town is selling the virtues of not being virtuous."

"It'd turn to ashes."

"All I want is, instead of watching soaps, for once I want to be in one. Can that be so bad?"

"It'd bring you unhappiness."

"How do you know?"

"Alma said so."

"Who's he?"

"C'mon, Shirley, you know who he is."

"Is he from Shakespeare?"

"He's from the Book of Mormon."

"And he talked about that?"

"He said wickedness was never happiness. I'll let you read it yourself. Where's your Book of Mormon?"

"I don't know. It's around somewhere—maybe in a box of books I've never unpacked."

"Have you ever read it?"

"Not all of it, but I've read parts."

"You mean you go to church every week and you've never even read the Book of Mormon?"

"No, but I believe it's true."

"Scrud! That makes me mad!" I roared, pounding my fist on her kitchen table. Unfortunately the impact knocked over a vase sitting on the edge and it shattered.

"Gee, I'm really sorry." I knelt down and began picking up the pieces.

She started laughing. "You cursed, Sam. You know that? You cursed and then you broke my vase. I'm going to tell the bishop. 'Bishop, you've got to change my home teacher. He comes into my home at midnight, curses, and breaks vases.'"

"Shirley, please read the Book of Mormon from cover to cover."

"What difference will it make? I'll still have these 'secret yearnings.'"

I dropped the pieces in her wastebasket. "Will you quit saying that?"

"Why? It was on one of the movie posters."

"You're making me nervous."

"Well," she smiled, "at least that's something."

"Look, I'll make a deal with you. Jon and I will come here every Friday night and talk with you about what you've read during the week, and then we'll take you out for a salad bar supper—if you promise to read ten pages a day."

"You and Jon will both take me out every weekend?" she asked.

"Yes, but no flirting with disaster."

"Who's he?" she teased.

"I'm not leaving till you promise."

She grinned mischievously at me. "Give me a couple of years to think about it."

"C'mon, Shirley. This is serious."

"Okay, it's a deal. Now you'd better go before the neighbors start flattering me with gossip."

We returned to the living room and I kicked Jon in his cowboy boots. He got up and walked like a zombie to the car.

She stopped me on my way out. "Sam?"

"Yes?"

"Let me hear you curse one more time," she smiled.

*   *   *   *   *   *

The three of us were talking about Third Nephi in the Book of Mormon.

"After his ressurection, Jesus visited the people in North or South America. After a few hours, he said he had to go visit others, but he saw how sorry they were to have him leave, and his heart went out to them. He asked if they had any sick or lame or blind or lepers, and they brought them to him, and one by one he healed them. Later the children were brought to him, and with them all about, he knelt down and prayed. It says that nobody can conceive of the joy they felt to hear Jesus pray for

50

them. Then he stood up, and took each child individually, one by one, and blessed them and prayed to Father in heaven for each one."

We were all quiet as we thought about that. Finally, Shirley said, "I wish I'd been there."

"Do you think he loved any of them more than he loves you?"

"He loves me too, doesn't he?" she asked.

"If you'd been the only one to benefit by it, he still would have come to earth and suffered and been crucified—if only for you, he would have done it all."

"Where does it say that?" Jon asked, always ready for a debate.

"I don't know—it's just a feeling I have," I admitted. "This church is his church, and when we remember him, then miracles happen. Mormons are professionals in doing things because somebody is going to make a report about it. We all want to look good for the report. But the Savior is the real reason we should try to help each other. And that's why we should live the commandments. Because if we don't, we'll disappoint the Savior. I don't want to do that."

"I don't either," Shirley said. I understood.

We finished the chapter, then headed out for a salad.

"Sam, I love the Book of Mormon. Why do we become so fascinated with frog stories when there's so much in the scriptures?"

"When we quit focusing on the Savior, we're left with frogs in buckets, and we think it's the gospel, but it isn't."

"Well, I feel terrific now," she said as we pulled in front of the restaurant. Jon was, of course, driving.

"Me too," I said.

"But in a way nothing's really happened. I'm still in the same boat. I may never get married."

"That's true."

"So the Savior can't make everything right, can he?"

"No, but he can help us get through whatever happens."

"Well, I'm not going to stay single," Jon added out of the blue.

Chapter Six

I was one of six single adult representatives in the ward. One Sunday we asked to meet with all the single adults after Sunday School. We asked them what suggestions they had for the single adult program.

A sister began. "The priesthood leaders think of the single adult program as just a way to get us all married off—a church dating bureau."

"And I don't care about your dances either," another lady said. "I've got a daughter at home who sees me only three hours a day because of my work, and I'm not leaving her just to sit in the corner and drink Kool-Aid."

"When I go to some of the dances," a young adult sister added, "I feel like I'm being graded like a pot roast in a meat market."

"I'm not at all interested in marriage," a middle-aged widower said, "but if we could have a service project where we actually helped people, then I could get interested in that."

We talked about several possible service projects.

"Why don't we be clowns and visit the kids in the hospital?"

For some reason the idea caught fire. Before we closed, we had three committees organized with a follow-up meeting set for the next week.

Within two weeks we began working on costumes. We

found a retired clown and asked him to meet with us and teach us.

Sister Hilton became the master of ceremonies, while I, with banjo, became Wilbur, an over-confident abrasive clown. Even Jon and Shirley worked out a routine together.

After rehearsing for a month, we tried out our act at a ward party and received enough laughs to encourage us to continue. We made arrangements to visit the children's ward of a hospital once a week.

I can't say what our visits did for the kids there—at least most of them laughed—but I know what they did for us. We would never be the same again. We learned to love them, and loving them helped us forget our own problems.

*　　　*　　　*　　　*　　　*　　　*

One evening in March, Shirley invited me to talk with her. I took Adam with me and let him rearrange her living room while we talked.

"Jon took me skiing yesterday," she said.

"How was the snow?"

"Good—three inches of new powder."

"Adam, don't turn on the TV," I warned. "How many times did you go down the run?"

"Once."

Adam had, of course, turned on the TV. I went over and pulled the plug.

"Once?"

"We would have gone more," she smiled, "but on top of the hill the first time, he asked me to marry him. After we got to the bottom, we wanted to talk, so we went inside the lodge and drank hot chocolate the rest of the afternoon."

"What did you tell him?"

"I said I had to talk to my home teacher first."

"That's me," I said.

"Yes. What do you think? Oh, before you say, Jon has a message for you. He said if you tell me not to marry him, he'll break both your legs."

"Macho—real macho. Ask him if he wants to play any more racquetball."

"He also said to tell you he loves me very much."

"Jon said that?" I asked. "He actually used the word *love*?"

"He can be very tender."

"You're kidding."

"So what do you think?"

"Shirley, why are you asking me? You're a big girl now—emotionally, that is."

"I'm asking you so you have a part in it."

"Marry him! He'll make a good husband and a terrific father. In fact, I may mail my son to you both. He's into the terrible twos now. Yesterday he took off his shirt and coated his body with peanut butter."

She laughed. "What did you do?"

"I got two pieces of bread and threatened to make a sandwich out of him."

I hugged her and wished her well.

"Do you have any advice for us?" she asked.

"Advice? Oh sure . . .There were these two frogs, and they both got caught in this bucket of cream . . ."

*　　*　　*　　*　　*　　*

Jon and Shirley were married in the temple in May. I was with them when they were sealed together as husband and wife for time and eternity. They were dry-eyed, but I wasn't.

Our clown project took off in the late spring. Suddenly we were in demand. We asked Sister Hilton to be our booking agent, and she kept busy juggling the calendar to accommodate the requests for us to appear at ward parties and service clubs.

After one of our performances, she made a presentation of her palm tree to the children's wing of the hospital.

"To tell you the truth," she said to me afterwards, "I don't even have time to water it anymore."

I continued to home teach Paul, our mild-mannered graduate student. All through February and March he had studied for a written exam over course work. He passed it, and then the next hurdle was an oral exam over course work, and then research. He kept busy, so when we visited him, we didn't stay long.

About the only thing I did for Joan was to babysit for her once a week so she could bowl with some friends from work.

In June, Jon, Shirley, and I launched our boat for the first time—it floated. That's always good news for a boat.

In late June, they said they were going to Yellowstone Park for a few days' vacation.

"Come along with us, Sam," Shirley said.

"Sure," I smiled, "that's just what newlyweds need—a home teacher along with them."

"Well, it's what you need. You need to get away."

"I'm getting along fine."

"Yes, but you're stale. C'mon, it'll be fun to have you along."

"What about nights?"

"You get a tent and we'll get a tent."

"It's a dumb idea, Shirley."

"No it isn't. You're part of our family, so come along."

"He'll come," Jon said emphatically. "We'll be leaving Monday, so be ready."

Adam and I went with them. On the way, as Jon drove, I sat in the back seat with Adam and went through all my banjo songs. Every two hours I offered to drive, but Jon was never tired. Jon never gets tired driving. He told us some hunting stories that were impossible to believe. Jon can make a simple thing like walking into the woods and shooting a deer seem like an epic adventure.

By late afternoon we were in the park and found a

camping site. I had a new tent and had trouble setting it up, so I just looked inept until Jon came over and put it up for me. I knew he would. Around him I practiced what could be called Studied Incompetence. If you played your cards wrong, Jon would do everything.

After supper we had a bonfire and roasted marshmallows. Adam loved them, especially the ones that caught fire and turned black.

Then it was night, and Jon took a trip while Shirley and I talked. Then Jon returned and Shirley made the same trip. When she returned, we all gazed into the embers of the fire while Jon told stories about grizzly bears ripping the arms off campers. Then he announced he was going to bed.

Jon left. A minute later, Shirley yawned and said, "I think I might go to bed now too—if that's all right."

"Oh sure," I smiled. "It was a long trip and I'll bet you're tired."

"You'll be okay here?" she asked.

"I'll be okay. You go ahead."

I smiled at her and she smiled back.

"Goodnight, Sam."

"Goodnight, Shirley."

"Shirl!" Jon called out, a little impatient. "You coming to bed or not?"

She left quickly.

I sat by the fire with Adam asleep in my lap, and looked at the dying embers. I was alone and Jon and Shirley were together. As much as we cared about each other, I would always be on the outside of their closeness.

I could make it alone if I had to. It might not be the way I wanted, but I could make it alone. I had my friends—the other clowns. I loved the single adults.

I put Adam in his sleeping bag and then decided to take a little walk down by the shore of Yellowstone Lake.

As I stood there, I started to talk to Charly very softly.

"Charly, I miss you. I wish you could be here tonight and we could talk. Charly, I want to get married again. I thought you ought to know. You knew about Elizabeth, but that was before I was really ready to love again—but now I am. If the right girl comes along, I will. And if I do, I'm not going to hold back because of you. That's the way it has to be. And after we're all on the other side, then we'll work out things between the three of us. Anyway, I thought you should know."

A falling star flashed across the sky.

"Charly, does that mean you approve—or that you don't approve?"

"I approve," a voice called out.

I turned to face two young couples who had been watching me talk to the sky. They burst out laughing.

I walked past them quickly, embarrassed.

"Charlie, are you out there?" one of them mimicked. The others burst out laughing.

The trouble with people today is that they have precious little respect for someone who talks to himself in the middle of the night.

I returned to camp, changed Adam's diaper, and went to bed.

Chapter Seven

It was summer and the night of the major league all-star game, and also the night for the stake single adult committee meeting.

In the spirit of pioneer sacrifice, I left the TV and walked to the meetinghouse, listening to the game on my old portable radio. It was a scruffy-looking model but it worked, except the back cover fell off with the slightest jar.

We held our meetings in the high council room. When I arrived, the only person in the room was a new female representative from another ward. I knew at once she was a returned missionary because of her short, easily kept hair style and her white blouse buttoned to the top, accented with a scarf around her neck.

She looked up as I entered, and I, with radio to my ear, nodded politely and sat down on the far end of the long table, about fifteen feet from her, and continued listening to the game.

It was the bottom of the eighth inning and the score was tied.

As time passed, most of the guys on the committee sat near me, and we all listened to the game.

Finally it was the bottom of the ninth, my team was one run behind, with two men on and one away.

The stake clerk came into the room and announced that our high councilor on the committee wouldn't be able to attend because his wife had just gone into labor. He asked if I would conduct the meeting.

"Why don't we wait a minute for the game to end?" I asked. "Is that all right with everyone?"

"I think we should begin now," the new girl said.

To this day I'm not sure I heard her say anything. I turned up the radio. The batter hit a single into shallow center field. Three men were on with only one away.

During a station break while they changed pitchers, the new representative walked over to where we were sitting. "If we say a meeting is going to start at seven-thirty, then I think it should start at seven-thirty."

The next batter hit a long fly ball into right field. It was caught on the warning track. Two men out. The next batter went to a full count. Time out because somebody threw some trash on the field.

"If we can't set a good example for promptness as a stake committee, how can we expect the same from the wards?"

I didn't hear a word she said.

"Now as we resume the game, the count is three balls, two strikes, the bases loaded—here's the windup, and the pitch . . ."

She turned off my radio!

"Doesn't anybody care about promptness?"

Two of us dived to turn on the radio, proceeding instead to knock it off the table. I ran to the other side of the table, only to see the back cover off and batteries scattered over the floor.

I fell to my knees and frantically began stuffing the batteries inside. One was missing. I crawled under the table to look for it.

"I'm sorry about your radio!" she called out, looking at me under the table.

Then she crawled under the table with me, searching and apologizing at the same time.

"It's just that time is so valuable, do you know what I mean? Time's all we have, isn't it? That's one of the most important lessons from my mission."

I stopped searching to stare at her.

It's Charly! I thought with a sudden leap of emotion. Who else would be crazy enough to be under a high council table with me.

She found the missing battery and gave it to me. I continued to stare at her as though she came from another planet.

"Are you going to turn it on now?" she asked.

"You mean my charm?" I said, nearly giggling.

"Sam!" someone yelled. "For crying out loud, turn on the radio!"

I slipped the battery in the radio.

"In all my years covering baseball, I don't ever recall a play like that last one!"

"What play?" somebody yelled.

"The technical director for this broadcast has been Morris Selmyers . . ."

"*What play?*"

"So on behalf of the CBS network . . ."

It was over and we didn't know the score.

I was still grinning at her. She smiled back politely and left me.

I crawled out, stood up, and found myself staring at her again. She had light brown hair with a slightly reddish tint. There were hundreds of curls—I imagined that when she washed her hair all she did to dry off was shake her head like a cocker spaniel. She had a long, graceful, Audrey Hepburn neck, partially obscured by a scarf that added some color to the creamy white embroidered blouse she was wearing. Her face was very nice—its most appealing features were her brown eyes and a summer's crop of freckles.

Maybe she's like Charly, I thought.

She broke the spell by walking down to pick up a clipboard and returning to say, "Well, I guess we can get started on our meeting now, can't we."

Oh rats, I moaned inwardly, she's efficient.

I asked someone to pray. After that I realized I had no idea what business to cover. I asked for the minutes to be read, hoping to get a clue.

60

"Margaret's not here and she has the minute book."

"Well," I stammered, "I'm not sure exactly what Brother Hammond had in mind for us to talk about tonight."

Silence.

"Did he talk to anyone about what he wanted us to cover?"

Silence—lowered heads.

"I've taken the liberty of drawing up a tentative agenda," the new girl said.

"Oh? What's your name?"

"Lara Whyte. I'm the young adult representative from Second Ward. I just returned from a mission to New Mexico. I'm originally from Idaho, but I'm working in Salt Lake City and staying with my aunt."

"Well, Sister Whyte, we'd like to welcome you to our meeting."

"I apologize for ruining your baseball game."

She handed me her clipboard with the agenda on it.

"Well," I said, "since Sister Whyte has been kind enough to provide us with an agenda, I guess we can proceed." I stopped talking, not believing the first item on the agenda. "Let's see, the first item is . . . Christmas customs in New Mexico. Uh, is that right, Sister Whyte? Is this an agenda I'm reading?"

"Yes, it is," she said calmly.

"I see—Christmas customs in New Mexico. Uh . . . what do you mean by that, Sister Whyte?"

She stood and cleared her throat. Her hand nervously went to her scarf as she began. "Well, as I explained, I just returned from a mission to New Mexico. They have a wonderful Christmas custom there that'd be so worthwhile for us to start here. What they do is take a little paper bag, pour a little sand in it, then stick a candle in the sand and light it. They might have hundreds of these on their lawns, outlining their sidewalks, or even on the roof. The whole town looks like a little fairy castle. I think we should do something like that as a single adult project for Christmas."

One of the guys on the committee started laughing.

"You want us to put candles in sacks and set them on fire?"

You're not Charly, I thought sadly.

"Oh no, the sack doesn't burn, just the candle. I know it doesn't sound like much, but it's beautiful."

"By any chance," one of the guys joked, "does your father manufacture either bags or sand or candles?"

"Or sell fire insurance?" another joked.

"It's a beautiful custom."

Definitely not Charly, I thought. She's a returned lady missionary with a clipboard. Either she was a pain to her supervising elders because she always complained, or else a pain to all the elders because she outperformed them in missionary work.

"Thank you," I said, carefully trying to avoid telling her how dumb I thought her idea was. "That was certainly an interesting suggestion, wasn't it. And we'll certainly want to give it more study. Since Christmas is five months away, maybe we could appoint a committee to look into it. Dave and Chuck, will you study her suggestion about burning bags for Christmas?"

"Oh, we sure will," Dave said with a grin.

I glanced at the rest of her agenda. The second item was "Bread." Somehow I knew she wanted everyone to stop eating white bread and start with whole wheat bread—no doubt causing the entire stake single adult group to develop problems with gas.

The third item was "Scripture Bowl." I knew she wanted us to sponsor a scripture chase, just so she could demonstrate her skill. Only thinking of herself with no consideration for the interests of the group. How selfish.

No, you're not Charly.

The fourth item was "Journals." I pictured a seminar in which she read boring passages from her life.

Suddenly I was mad at her for not being Charly, and for her dumb ideas, and for talking so freely at her first council meeting instead of respectfully listening for a few months the way most of the other women on the committee did.

I certainly wasn't going to plod through the rest of her dumb agenda.

"We certainly want to thank Sister Wheat . . ."

"It's Whyte, not Wheat," she corrected.

" . . . for her input tonight. She's only been here a short time and look at what she's done already."

Two of the more avid baseball fans grumbled about what she'd done.

"Thank you, Sister Whyte, for your suggestions."

"If you want, you may call me Lara."

"If it's all the same, I'll call you Sister Whyte," I replied coolly.

By setting my notebook on her agenda, I managed to bury it. "There are some items we should cover. I think it'd be nice if we sponsored a single adult racquetball tournament."

The rest of the meeting went smoothly. Sister Whyte contented herself with keeping notes. In an hour we had finished.

After the meeting, she stayed behind to finish her notes while I talked to Dave about the size of the trophies for our racquetball tournament. Then he left and she and I were alone.

"You don't seem very interested in new ideas," she said, still writing.

"On the contrary, we always like new ideas. That's how we progress."

"Why were you staring at me under the table?"

"I'm sorry. I thought at first that you were like someone I used to know, but I was wrong. You aren't anything like that person."

"Later in the meeting I felt you turned very cold toward me. If we're going to work together on this committee, we should get along. Why don't you like me?"

"Sister Whyte, I don't even know you enough not to like you. But I'm sure with time—" I shook my head. "I'm sorry—that's not what I meant."

"Is it because you didn't get along with lady missionaries on your mission?"

That seemed a better explanation than the real one. "Yes, that's it."

"Well, I don't suppose I'll get much done with you in charge of the committee."

"You want us all to bake bread in unison with you, don't you," I snapped.

"Why are you so mad at me?"

"I'm not mad. There's no reason for me to be mad at you, and so I'm not mad."

"Then please lower your voice."

"Sister Whyte, I'm going home now, but I'm leaving you with a compliment. You have nice hair. I like the short little curls."

"Thank you," she said, softening a bit.

"I'll bet you don't even have to curl it, do you. All you do is concentrate real hard and it does whatever you want, doesn't it. Well, you'll find that's one difference between your hair and me. Good night, Sister Whyte."

*   *   *   *   *   *

A day later I felt rotten for insulting her. That's the trouble with a conscience—it keeps bugging you. I decided to phone and apologize.

"Sister Whyte, this is Sam Roberts. I was the one under the table last night."

She laughed. "I hope nobody's listening in on this conversation."

"I called to apologize for being so rude."

"I accept. Now it's my turn. I apologize for being so impatient with you."

Pause.

"I guess we've cleaned the slate, haven't we," she said.

"I guess so. Can we talk for a few minutes to fill it with things we won't have to erase again?"

A minute later we got on the subject of our missions.

"You know," she said, "that reminds me of something

that happened on my mission. We'd been tracting all day, and it was time to quit, but there were just four more houses on the block, so I suggested we finish. On the last house we met a wonderful family. We taught them, and four weeks later they were baptized—a wonderful family of six."

"Six—how nice," I said politely. "But your story reminds me of something that happened on my mission. We were out tracting and there was a house with a big fence and a sign that read 'Beware of Dog.' I told my companion we weren't going to let a little dog stop us. So we opened the gate and the dog came over and jumped him. I went ahead and knocked on the door while he wrestled with the dog. I met the nicest family there. They called off the dog and let us in. In a few weeks they were all baptized—a family of seven."

"How nice," she said politely. "My family of six has been such an asset to the Church. He's a bishop now."

"Oh, a bishop," I said, outwardly delighted. "That's nice."

"Is the family you baptized still active in the Church?" she asked.

"Oh yes—he's the custodian of a very large chapel. You know, a good custodian is worth so much these days—maybe even more than a bishop."

"Not only is he a bishop," she continued, "but they in turn invited their friends to learn about the Church. Last time I checked, four other families had joined from their efforts."

I would not be defeated. Secretly though, I loved the challenge.

"A custodian is the hub around which a ward rotates."

"And from those families, there are now two missionaries serving. Who knows how many they've baptized by now."

"An excellent custodian can save the Church thousands of dollars each year by doing routine maintenance himself. For instance, my custodian does his own periodic boiler upkeep."

"Is that good?" she asked.

"Oh my, yes. Not only that, who can put a price on the value to missionary work of a well-kept lawn and flowers? Do you know how many people join the Church each year just because they drive by our buildings and think, 'I ought to join that church—they keep up their lawn.' Do you?"

"No, I don't," she confessed. "How many?"

A long pause. "I don't know either—but I'm sure we'd both be surprised by how many there are."

I started to laugh. "I surrender! You topped me—this time."

"Can you come over?"

"Well, I don't know. If I came over, I might get to like you. That'd be too bad, wouldn't it? We were getting to be such good enemies."

"If you want, we can sit under my aunt's kitchen table. So far, that's been the only time you've been very friendly."

"Why not?" I said. "I've still got a family of ten I haven't used yet."

"Give me an hour to get ready."

The reason I like her, I thought as I shaved, is she's a challenge. That turned out to be one of the great understatements of my life.

An hour later when I rounded a corner, I saw twenty paper bags glowing in the dark along the sidewalk to her house. She was sitting on the porch waiting for me.

"Have any trouble finding the house?" she teased as I walked up the glowing sidewalk.

"Sorry for making fun of your idea—they look great."

She showed me how to set one up—a small paper bag, a candle, a little sand or soil. "In New Mexico, they call them luminarios."

We went inside. I met her aunt, Sister Gillespie, a cheery lady who played the role of matchmaker.

We had grape juice and a slice of whole wheat bread. Then we played Pit, a game where everyone yells trying to trade off some cards. After the first game, Lara excused herself for a minute.

"She's a beautiful girl, isn't she."

"Yes, she is."

"And she's smart too, and a wonderful cook. She made the bread you know. And so spiritual."

I nodded as the sales pitch continued.

Then Lara returned and her aunt disappeared.

I played my trump card, the family of ten, and she didn't even try to top it. An hour later we walked out on her porch.

"I'd like to take you out tomorrow night."

"That would be nice," she said.

"Oh, one thing," I said, "in case you were wondering if I'm going to kiss you, I'm not."

"I wasn't wondering," she said.

Pause.

"You weren't?"

"I'm very selective about who I kiss."

"What I mean is, even if we date a lot, I probably won't ever kiss you."

"Fine," she said, apparently unconcerned.

I studied her. "Is that why you went on your mission?"

"What?"

"Oh, you know—some lady missionaries resent men. When I was a zone leader, we had several like that."

"What you mean is they didn't like you," she defended.

"They didn't like any men."

She laughed.

"Is this a trick to get me to kiss you, to prove I'm not a man hater."

"No trick," I said, suddenly serious. "It hasn't been that long since my wife died."

"I understand."

"I still love her. We were married in the temple, so we're still married. How's that for dumping cold water on things?"

"You're honest. I like that."

I reached out and held her hand. "How old are you?"

"Twenty-three."

"I'm twenty-seven."

"When you were in high school," she kidded, "I was still getting *The Weekly Reader*."

"It's fun talking to you, Lara."

I'd spent the evening admiring her face. The smooth, graceful neck and almost sculptured beauty of her face were offset by the down-home touch of her freckles. Looking into her eyes as I did then gave me the feeling of falling, like some wandering comet suddenly captured by the sun.

"I'd like to compliment you on your eyes," I said, still captured by them. "Since I've been married before, I know about the wonders of chemistry women use to look nice—you know, eyeliner, eye shadow, eye-coloring pencils, mascara. Still, I find a certain satisfaction in staring into your eyes."

"If that's a compliment," she grinned, "then thank you."

I escaped. "Well, good night, Sister Whyte. Don't forget to say your prayers."

"I won't—I'll pray for you."

"What for?"

"That you'll come by again."

"Tomorrow night?"

"My prayers are answered," she smiled.

"Can I ask you a personal question? Is there anything wrong with your neck?"

"No, why?"

"Well, that scarf around your neck. It's July, you know. I thought you might be hiding some sort of scar."

"Just a habit from my mission, I guess. Here, I'll show you."

She pulled off her scarf, revealing the rest of her attractive neck.

"Oh sure, a regular neck. Thanks."

"Good night, Sam."

"Good night, Sister Whyte."

She shook her head. "That won't do anymore."

"It won't?"

"Now that you've seen my neck, you'd better call me Lara."

"Good night—Lara."

"Good night, Sam."

Chapter Eight

The next day I dropped by at seven. She wasn't ready, so her aunt continued the Lara Lectures.

"She's so healthy. And her teeth—ask to see her teeth sometime."

Lara showed up and we looked at a newspaper to see about a movie. We ruled out the R's, marked out the PG's with obviously lurid titles. I'd already seen the G's. Finally we were left with three PG's.

She had a magazine that rated movies; she looked up the three in question.

"Well," she said, "they're basically all right, except for a little nudity."

"A little nudity?" I asked. "Does that mean little in time or in area of body exposed?"

She smiled and shook her head. "No movie—right?"

"Right. I'm still reeling from seeing your neck."

After a couple of games of Pit with her aunt, I asked Lara if we could drop by and see Paul. He'd taken his Ph.D. comprehensive course work exam that day and I wanted to see how he'd done.

"I passed!" he shouted as he opened the door. We sat down while he gave us a question-by-question playback. I didn't understand a word he was saying, but I knew he was happy.

"You should celebrate tonight—let us buy you a treat."

We drove to my favorite ice cream store. I suggested we all get banana splits.

"Not for me, thank you," Lara said. "I don't eat anything with refined sugar in it."

She's a strange one, I thought.

"Well, what would you like?"

"Could I have just a plain banana?"

"So what's wrong with refined sugar?" I asked after the waitress left.

"It's not good for the body."

"Don't you ever have anything sweet?" I asked.

"Oh sure—I make a little candy with honey, raisins, and wheat germ."

Inwardly I groaned.

"But it's paid off. I've never had a cavity."

"I've heard that—can I see your teeth?"

"You've seen my neck—that should be enough."

"C'mon, your aunt promised me."

She gave me a warm smile, but I forgot to look at her teeth.

A few minutes later our food came. Paul and I dug into our banana splits while Lara peeled her banana.

"All I have left now in school," Paul said eagerly, "is a little more research, then writing the dissertation."

"And then what?"

"Get a job someplace—maybe Bell Labs in New Jersey."

"What about marriage?" I asked.

"There'll be time for that after my dissertation."

"Not many LDS girls in New Jersey. You'd better spend time on it before you leave."

He considered that for a few spoonfuls. "You're right—I should get married before I leave Utah. Who do I see about that?"

"See?" Lara asked. "First you have to start dating."

"I don't know anybody."

"How about in your ward?"

"I'm the assistant clerk, so it's not like I'm a stranger to the girls in the ward. After all, my name's on all their donation receipts."

Lara and I looked at each other.

"Paul," Lara suggested, "I know a girl who goes to the U. She works part-time in our store. I think I can talk her into going out with you—once."

"I've never been on a date. What do I do?"

"Well," Lara said, "you can always take her to a movie."

". . . with just a little nudity," I added.

"What?" Paul asked, now even more worried.

"Or," Lara reconsidered, "you can take her to dinner."

"Alone?" he asked. "Do I have to be alone with her?"

*   *   *   *   *   *

A week later we arranged to have Paul and his date to dinner at Lara's place.

Her aunt left the house as we finished the preparations for the evening. Paul nervously paced back and forth as Lara and I set the table.

"What do I say to her?" he asked, wiping his forehead with a linen napkin from the table, then tossing it back on a plate.

"Talk about the weather," I suggested, placing the napkin back in place.

"Oh, sure." He sighed with relief, but then panicked again. "Tell me something to say about the weather."

"It's hot for this time of year," I suggested.

"Thanks."

The doorbell rang and Lara got it. Julie came bouncing in. She was a sophomore in Physical Education—blonde, and energetic.

"Sorry I'm late! Our game went into extra innings, but we won!"

"Julie," Lara said, "this is Paul and this is Sam."

"Hi, Julie," I said. "Lara's told me a lot about you."

Paul shook her hand in a stiff missionary style. "It's

certainly a pleasure to be here today." Then, almost ominously, he added, "Everybody's talking about you."

She flinched just a little but then smiled.

Lara interceded. "Why don't you sit down and I'll get us something to nibble on while the casserole cooks."

Lara left and the party ground to a halt.

"Well, here we are," Julie said warmly.

Seconds ticked by.

"Yes, we are—we're here," Paul said desperately.

More dead time broken by Paul blurting, "I'm hot for this time of year."

"Oh, sure," she agreed.

We were saved by Lara bringing in some dip and a bowl of potato chips.

"How nice," Julie bubbled. She tasted the dip. "This is delicious! What is it, Lara?"

"A shrimp and clam dip. One of my aunts taught me how to make it before she passed away."

"How soon before?" Paul asked, eyeing the dip suspiciously.

We ignored him. I tried some and liked it.

Paul tried but in the process knocked the bowl onto the carpet.

"Oh, no!" he moaned, falling to his knees and scooping up the dip in his hands and plopping the mess on the coffee table. Then he tried to wipe his hands with the cloth on the coffee table, managing to spill the chips too.

While he apologized over and over again, Lara ran to get a rag and I picked up the chips. In a minute, it was all cleaned up.

"Paul," Julie said, "can I give you a little advice? You seem so tense. You need to learn to relax your body."

"Relax?" Paul croaked, his voice at least an octave above normal. "My body has just destroyed Lara's dead aunt's chip dip, and you ask me to relax? My body feels like it's made out of stiff cardboard."

"Let me teach you an exercise that'll help," Julie said. "Just lean back and relax." She rearranged Paul's head against the back of the swivel rocker, then encouraged

Lara and me to sit on the couch and follow along.

"Okay, are we all ready? First thing, everybody relax your toes. Think of calmness flowing over your toes."

Paul sat up. "It turns out my toes are never very tense."

"It's okay, just sit back. Now let's all relax our ankles. Concentrate on your ankles. Paul, are your ankles relaxed? Okay—now relax your legs. Do you feel the relaxing essence flowing into your legs?"

She waited a few seconds. "Now let's all relax our lower trunks. Think of the calming essence flowing into your lower trunks."

Paul suddenly stood up.

"What's wrong?" Julie asked.

"I have to go to the bathroom." He left, opening doors at random until he found the bathroom.

Lara shook her head and started to laugh. "Julie, I'm sorry about this. You're being such a good sport. Can you hold out through dinner?"

"I sense such potential in him, don't you?" Julie said.

"You're kidding?" I asked.

In a minute, Paul returned and sat down, his back still ramrod straight. Lara went to check on the food. Julie stood behind Paul's chair and massaged his neck and shoulder muscles.

"You have very strong shoulder muscles."

"That's from doing this," he said, shrugging his shoulders.

"Does this feel good?"

"Oh yes—very good."

"Tell me about yourself," she said.

"I'm an assistant clerk."

"Really? My father was a stake clerk before my parents left on their mission."

"My parents are gone this year too. My dad works for an oil company. If your father were here, do you know what I'd do? I'd ask him about my PF-19 report."

"He'd help you. He's very good at reports."

Paul's eyes were partially closed as Julie massaged his

shoulders. "You know, if the other secretaries'd just get their reports in on time, a clerk's job'd be a lot easier."

"That's just what Daddy used to say."

Next Julie began to massage his scalp.

"You have a very loose scalp."

Paul opened his eyes and looked worried. "You mean it might fall off?"

"Oh no—it's good to have a loose scalp. People with tight scalps go bald. Here, reach up and move it around. See, it moves."

"How about that!" Paul exclaimed. "It really is loose, isn't it! Sam, do you have a loose scalp?"

"I don't know."

"Julie, see if he does."

She tested my scalp with her fingers. "It's loose, but not as loose as yours, Paul."

"Isn't that wonderful about my scalp?" Paul grinned.

"I always test the scalps of the guys I date, and I don't remember anyone with a looser scalp than yours."

"How about that!" he said proudly.

Watching them, I had the feeling I was in a foreign country.

"And," Julie continued, "your nose. I've made noses my hobby. I even have a nose scrapbook—I like your nose."

"My nose too?" Paul said, almost unable to contain his delight. "I hardly think about it—except when I have a cold."

He was now touching his nose, feeling its shape, moving it from side to side. It was gross to watch.

"You've really neglected your body, haven't you."

"I concentrated on my mind."

"And I've concentrated on the body. There's so much we could teach each other, isn't there. Tell me, do you ever get any exercise—swimming, for instance?"

"Oh sure, I swim. I'm an Eagle Scout."

"You're an Eagle Scout?" she asked in awe. "That's so wonderful! Tell me some other things about yourself."

"Sometimes I go swimming on campus. I like to submerge and sit motionless on the bottom of the pool."

"No kidding! I go swimming all the time. Wait! I think I've seen you on the bottom!"

"I went last Thursday."

"I saw you! I asked the lifeguard to check if you'd drowned. Do you remember seeing me there?"

"Without my glasses, I can't see anything."

He was still touching his nose. "Can I ask you a personal question?"

"I guess so."

"What do you do about nose hairs?"

I escaped to the kitchen. Lara was a flurry of efficiency.

"How's it going in there?" she asked.

"You wouldn't believe it—we've created a monster."

"Things are about ready here," she said.

"Lara, do you like to cook?"

"Sure—why?"

"Just wondering."

On my way back I swiped an olive.

Julie was massaging Paul's scalp again. His glasses were off, his eyes were closed, and he was very relaxed.

"I went on a mission to Nebraska," he said slowly.

"Tell me about it."

"Well, it's mostly rural, you know."

"Oh?"

"Yes, they have farms and ranches in Nebraska. More farms in eastern Nebraska, but more ranches in western Nebraska."

"How do they ever decide on something like that?"

"I think it depends on the type of soil."

"Oh sure, it would, wouldn't it. You're so smart."

"Now you tell me about yourself," Paul asked.

"Well, I'm a PE major—let's see—I teach the family relations class in Sunday School."

"I think family relations are important—especially to a family," Paul said drowsily.

"That's so true. Some couples, before they get married, don't sit down and talk about important things —like how many children they want."

"I want as many as my wife and I can stand—I mean handle."

"Oh, I agree."

"You do?"

"And we're taught that communications are important to a marriage. A husband and wife should be able to talk—well, like we are tonight."

There was magic between them. Here they were, involved in one of the all-time dumb conversations, yet there were sparks flying between them.

"Paul, you know so much. I've never known a scientist before," she said, finishing her scalp massage and sitting down near him.

"I know the laws that govern matter and energy. Because of that, I understand the universe."

"Well, that's quite a lot, isn't it?" Julie said. "I don't know that much, but I do know the rule for all games involving a ball—you know, football, baseball, volleyball."

"Since you're in Physical Education, maybe you can help me. My mother says I walk like a duck. My own mother! You can imagine what strangers say. Can you help me?"

"Sure I will. C'mon," she said, pulling him to his feet.

They walked slowly out the living room with Julie making sure his feet pointed straight ahead. In a minute they were back.

"Sam, look at my feet!"

They left again, taking a route through the dining room into a hall and back to the living room.

"Of course," Julie said on their return trip, "we have an advantage, being members of the Church. Starting with a temple marriage, kneeling in the temple together, committing to love each other for time and eternity. Well, it's very important to me. I don't want anything less, do you?"

They were gone again.

"It hasn't been easy, has it," Julie said on the next trip, looking at his temple recommend. "Keeping yourself worthy—there are plenty of opportunities to go wrong in this life."

Paul stopped walking. "There are?"

Lara came into the living room. "Well, it's finally ready. I bet you've all been starving to death."

"Oh no," Paul said. "This has been one of the most interesting times of my life. In these few minutes, Julie's taught me how to walk and what to do with nose hairs."

Lara's mouth fell open.

Julie took Paul's arm and they walked grandly into the dining room with their feet straight ahead.

"If my mother could see me now!" Paul exclaimed.

Lara looked at me and I shrugged my shoulders.

"Lara," Julie asked, "did you know Paul is an Eagle Scout?"

"After supper," Paul confidently announced, "if you want, I'll teach you all semaphore signaling."

Chapter Nine

Lara and I were coming out of a concert. Parked beside my car was a Jaguar sports car. I stood and admired it.

"Commandment number ten," she joked. "Thou shalt not covet."

A few blocks later, I asked how she knew it was the tenth of the Ten Commandments.

"Oh," she said, a little embarrassed, "it's just a little memory trick I use. It's really nothing."

"I'm interested—tell me about it."

Her face clouded over. "It's really kind of dumb. You don't really want me to bore you with it."

"C'mon, I'm curious."

"I'm not supposed to talk about it with someone I'm dating."

"Why not?"

"A guy has to feel superior around a girl, and if he doesn't, he leaves. That's what all my roommates in college, who are all married now, used to say."

"Oh c'mon, just tell me."

"All right. Commandment number one—think of one and only. Thou shalt have no other gods before me. Okay? One—one and only."

I nodded my head.

"Commandment number two—think of zoo. A zoo has statues of lions and tigers. Statues are graven images.

Commandment number two—think of zoo—Thou shalt not make unto thee any graven images. Got it?"

"Sure," I said nonchalantly, but feeling a little threatened.

"Commandment number three—think of tree. A tree has leaves, a leaf has veins. Commandment number three—Thou shalt not take the name of the Lord in vain.

"Commandment number four—think of door. A door has a keyhole, which reminds you of holy. Commandment number four—Thou shalt keep the Sabbath Day holy."

I was looking at her with my mouth wide open.

"Commandment number five—think of drive. Your parents are taking you out for a drive. Five—think of drive—think of parents. Commandment number five—Honor your father and mother."

"Commandment number six—think of sticks. You could kill somebody with a stick. Comandment number six—thou shalt not kill."

I felt a large drop of sweat roll down my arm.

"Commandment number seven—think of heaven. You can't go to heaven if you commit adultery and don't repent. Seven—think of heaven—you can't get there with adultery. Commandment number seven—Thou shalt not commit adultery.

"Commandment number eight—think of gate. You need gates to keep away robbers. Eight—think of gate—think of robbers. Commandment number eight—Thou shalt not steal."

"Oh sure," I said, my head whirling.

"Commandment number nine—think of lying. Thou shalt not bear false witness.

"Commandment number ten—think of hen. You wish you could have your neighbor's chicken. Ten—hen. Thou shalt not covet.

"It's so simple, isn't it?" she said enthusiastically. "On my mission I used the same idea to memorize scriptures. I found it was really easy to learn about five hundred scriptures that way."

"Oh," I said, wondering if I knew fifty scriptures.

"It's sort of a hobby. When I was in college I read this book, let's see—it was called *The Memory Book*. It taught all these little tricks. I got so every week I was memorizing a *Time* magazine."

I was getting a bad headache.

"Oh, you memorize *Time* magazines," I said numbly.

"It's really easy. I used to do it for my roommates, but they told me never to tell any guy I liked about it. They said it would intimidate him, and he'd never feel comfortable around me again. You're the first guy I've ever told. You don't feel intimidated, do you?"

"Oh, no," I said.

"Then why is your forehead sweating so much?"

"Okay, maybe a little. I had to have my mother sew the combination of my gym locker on the inside of my gym shorts."

"Well, silly, that's why I'm here. Just tell me the combination and I'll make up a little rhyme so you can remember it."

"I don't know it—it's in my gym shorts at home." I wiped my forehead. "I think your roommates were right."

"You feel intimidated?"

"It's like dating Albert Einstein."

"Sam, can't we be a team? I'll teach you things about memorizing and you teach me about racquetball and fishing. Is it a deal?"

"Deal," I said weakly, "reminds you of creel, which is what you need for fishing."

At that moment I'd have given anything to be with a girl whose greatest challenge in life so far had been passing her driver's exam.

*   *   *   *   *   *

The next day Lara went with me to a clown training session. We spent half an hour tumbling and learning to take falls. For practice we went outside the church and practiced walking into the flagpole, letting our feet strike the pole an instant before our heads touched it. With enough practice, it sounds like you've cracked your head very hard.

Then we worked out some standard clown dialogue and routines.

A day later I went to her house and spent fifteen enjoyable minutes looking into her eyes—applying clown makeup, creating a clown character.

"If you get any of that powder in my eyes, my contacts'll never be the same," she warned.

"I used to know a girl who wore contacts. The first time I kissed her, one of them fell out."

"Probably a poor fit."

"Could be it was just the thrill of kissing me."

"I doubt it," she teased. "I've worn these on the roller coaster, and they stayed on fine—and I doubt if kissing you beats that."

A minute later, she asked, "Sam, was that your wife you were talking about?"

"Yes."

"I thought so. You can tell me about her—I mean you don't have to hide her from me by saying 'a girl I once knew.' I know you've been married, and that you loved her, and you always will. Okay?"

"Thanks. Most people won't let me talk about her. When I start, they get nervous and tell me I have to start a new life now. I know that, but Lara, she was terrific. I want people to know about her. She was a good person, but she didn't intimidate anyone. Everybody loved her."

I talked about Charly. When I finished, Lara agreed Charly was one in a million. "But there's at least one person intimidated by her, and that's me. When we're together and we pass some place, like Liberty Park, and you quit talking and look very sad, I know you're thinking about her. Minutes slip by and I know I've lost you to her. After a while, you come back to me. Is it always going to be like that?"

"I don't know. She's still with me."

That dampened our conversation for a while. I applied a foundation of clown white to her face.

"Sam, do I intimidate you?"

"A little. The trouble with us is we're equal. Mission, college, work—I don't have an edge on you in anything."

"That threatens you?"

"A woman is supposed to—"

"Not compete with men?" she suggested.

"No, she can compete—it's just that she—"

"Shouldn't do better than men."

"Well, not exactly," I stammered. "You see, a woman has a certain role—"

"Being mediocre?"

"No, she can excel in certain areas."

"Making the bed, washing the dishes?"

"Lara, you know what the Church teaches. A woman's place is in the home, being a wife and mother."

"Terrific—I agree with that. But not every girl in the Church can guarantee she'll be asked by a worthy man, so she needs two possible paths in life. Being a wife and mother is the first priority for a Latter-day Saint woman, but the second is having a meaningful career. If she doesn't get married, you can't expect her to sit home and wait by the phone her whole life, can you?"

"I guess not."

"And even if she gets married, it'll be insurance for her to have a marketable skill in case her husband passes away and she has to raise the family alone."

"Okay."

"Good, I'm glad you agree, because I really like my job. Sure, it's only selling women's clothes in a store, but I'm very good at it. At first I was hired only as a part-time bookkeeper, but one day when someone was sick my boss, Steve, asked me to try selling. I did well from the start. And I've used my memory tricks to associate the names and faces of our regular customers. Now they ask for me when they come in. Steve keeps telling me I should start working Saturdays, but I've resisted, because then I couldn't be with you. But Sam, I'm good at what I do. I'm one of the best."

"But when you try to be the best, you compete with a man whose family depends on him."

"Then he'd better work harder, because I'm not letting up."

"What if somebody labels you as a pushy woman?"

"But you give the same traits to a man, and he's called a man with initiative."

"Okay, but let me ask you one question—do you support priesthood direction by a husband in a home?"

"I knew you were going to ask that. Yes, I do. Why? Is this a proposal?"

"No."

"Okay then, don't ask me to do less than my best in my job."

I decided to avoid the subject in the future.

"Do you speak German?"

"A little, why? Does that intimidate you too?"

"No, I'm turning you into Fran the Frazzled Fraulein." I finished by placing a ridiculous red wig on her head, with hair sticking out as though she'd been electrocuted. I started to laugh.

She stood up and looked in the mirror and burst out laughing too.

"That's the real me?"

"Yes," I grinned.

She practiced in front of the mirror and slowly became Fran with a rasping fractured English-German voice.

An hour later, we headed for the hospital to meet our friends and entertain the children.

First we went around individually to each child, showing them tricks or giving out crayons and coloring books. Then we gave a show in one of the large waiting rooms for those who were well enough to see it.

Afterwards we changed our clothes and took Adam to the zoo. On the way, he sat between us and made eyes at Lara. By the time we arrived, he was on her lap, being

84

cuddled by her and loving every minute of it. At the zoo, we visited the animals and Lara imitated the sounds of each one. A couple of times they answered her, sending Adam into giggles.

When he saw the elephants, he started running too fast and fell down, scraping his knees and arms. He stood up crying, ran toward us, ignored me, and fell into Lara's arms for love and comfort.

On the way home, he chanted, "My mommy, my daddy, my mommy."

Neither of us commented on the chant.

* * * * * *

Saturday we took Paul and Julie with us for some boating and fishing.

After an hour of buzzing around the lake, we anchored in a cove to try some fishing. Lara and I both took a nap while Paul taught Julie how to play chess.

After a while I woke up and checked the lines, then lay back down with my fishing cap over my face.

"Tell me again how the bishops move," I heard her say.

"Sideways," Paul answered.

"I knew a bishop once who moved like that—he was a little overweight." After a few seconds she said, "There, that's my move."

"Checkmate."

After a pause, she asked, "Tell me again what that means."

"It means I can take your king on the next move. The game's over."

"Over? Why? I still have plenty of others left. My queen can take over."

"When the king is gone, the game is over."

"I'll bet a man made up this game."

Paul laughed and it sounded relaxed and human. Being with Julie had helped him.

"Julie," he said enthusiastically, "look how blue the sky is."

"I know—isn't it beautiful!"

"I know why the sky is blue."

"Me too," she said. "Because that's the way Heavenly Father made it."

"I know another reason."

"What's the other reason?"

"The blue color of the sky is caused by the wavelength dependence of the scattering of sunlight by molecules in the atmosphere."

Silence, followed by, "I like my answer better."

"And do you see little blobs when you look at the sky?"

"What?"

"Little blobs, like little circles. When you blink, they move."

Seconds passed. "I see them! Some are in long chains. What are they?"

"Loose blood cells inside your eye floating around."

"Oh Paul, you're so smart. Tell me some more."

"Matter is made up of neutrons, protons, and electrons."

"I know electrons!" she exclaimed. "They make electricity!"

"That's right," Paul laughed.

"See, I'm not so dumb."

"I never thought you were. It's just we both have different areas we're smart in."

"Right—what else?"

"Neutrons and protons are themselves made up of quarks, and quarks are tied together with gluons."

"Like Elmer's Glue?" she asked.

"No, not exactly."

"Elmer's sticks so well. My mother broke a tea cup once and—"

"Quarks have properties like color, charm, and flavor."

She laughed. "Oh Paul, you're such a tease."

"I'm serious."

"It sounded as though you were talking about Life Savers. Oh Paul, I love to hear you explain things. You know everything."

"Not everything, but all I know I want to share with you. I care about you—very much."

She sighed, then became very serious. "Paul, there's something I need to talk to you about."

"If it's about changing the rules of chess, I don't think that's practical."

"It's not that—I should've told you this the first time we met. Paul, I'm waiting for a missionary."

There was a long pause as all the confidence she had built in him drained out. His voice cracked as he asked, "You are?"

"I met him last year before he left on his mission."

"Is he an athlete?"

"He played freshman football."

"A football player," he moaned, utterly demolished. "Sure—it figures. I should've known someone like you would be taken. Just my luck, isn't it. When I was five, I was the only kid who didn't find any Easter eggs. I guess you want me to quit seeing you, don't you."

"Just like that?" she asked, sounding very surprised.

"In life some people find the Easter eggs and some don't."

"I'm not an Easter egg," she said, sounding irritated with him.

"And I'm not a winner—but that must've been obvious from the beginning. What was I, Julie, an extra credit project? Well anyway, thanks for showing me how to walk."

They sat in silence. Paul folded up the chess set.

"What on earth do they teach you in physics?" she suddenly roared. "You don't know beans!"

"Like what?"

"Like the saying, 'When the going gets tough, the tough get going!'"

"Is that so? Did your jock boyfriend tell you that?" Paul exploded.

"No, but he could have. Believe me, he'd never give up just because a girl told him she was waiting for a missionary! No, sir! Especially if he cared about her. That'd only make him more determined to win her love. He'd never quit!"

A long pause, followed by Paul timidly asking, "He wouldn't?"

"No—not him. He's a guy who never gives up. Fourth down, twenty yards to go—he tries to run it. That's his style."

"What would he do?"

"He'd take me in his arms and tell me he loves me."

Paul gasped. "He would?"

"Sure—that's the kind of guy he is."

A few seconds later, Paul said, "Julie, I love you."

My hat was over my head so I couldn't see, but a few seconds later I heard Paul ask, "Is this okay the way I'm holding you?"

"Not so much around my neck—I can't breathe."

"Like that?"

"That's fine."

"Julie, I love you. How's that?"

"Then he'd kiss me."

I nudged my hat a little to see what was happening. Paul kissed her lightly, then broke away and burst out, "Wow! He sounds like a wonderful guy!"

He kissed her again.

"What's that saying again?" he asked after they broke apart.

"When the going gets tough, the tough get going."

The next kiss was even longer. I felt guilty for spying on them, and turned to look at Lara. She was also faking sleep, but I could see a mischievous grin on her face.

A minute later when Paul broke away, he enthusiastically cried out, "You know, we need to support our missionaries! Let's bake him some chocolate chip cookies!"

They kissed again.

My guilt runneth over, and I sat up and rattled around, but they didn't seem to hear. Finally I picked up a tackle box and dropped it on the floor of the boat. They broke away. Paul's face turned a crimson red.

"Julie was just telling me about the missionary she's waiting for."

"I see."

"We're going to bake him some chocolate chip cookies."

"The way you two were going, you won't need an oven."

Paul laughed with delight. "Well, you know what they say—when the going gets tough, the tough get going."

*   *   *   *   *   *

We had a picnic supper on the boat, and then around eight o'clock we went to shore. While Lara and Julie went off on some errand, Paul and I cleaned our fish.

"Okay, Paul, you put the knife here and slice until you get to the gills," I said, trying to teach him how to clean a fish.

"Kissing is a lot of fun, isn't it," he said, still in a daze.

"Did you see how I did that?" I asked.

"You know what, I never kissed before today. In high school, the only girl friend I had was Martha Swartz. We had calculus together. She was really into biology—her hands smelled of formaldehyde. I never kissed her—I was afraid I'd pass out from the formaldehyde and she'd add me to her bug collection."

"Paul, watch how I pull out the insides."

"Then there was the girl who sat next to me in band. She had the lowest body temperature of any person I've ever met. The guys in the trombone section, they were the rowdy ones, they used to come up and shake hands with her just to see how cold her fingers were."

"Now you take your thumb and run it up the spinal column to get rid of all the blood. Watch me, Paul."

"Actually," Paul continued, "except for a cousin in

the ninth grade, Julie is the first real girl I've kissed. Not that I've kissed any fake girls. Once I almost kissed a girl on the cover of the *New Era*, but that doesn't count."

I sighed. "Paul, do you want to clean a fish?"

"No, you go ahead. It'd make my hands smell. I need to keep my hands smelling good—that's one thing I learned from Martha Swartz."

I put the knife down. Paul was looking at the lake and daydreaming. "Okay, Paul, you've discovered kissing. But look, you can't kiss all the time or it'll lead to trouble."

"Trouble?"

"Yes, trouble," I answered ominously.

He looked at me as though he didn't know what I was talking about.

"You have to be careful."

·"Gosh, Sam, I'm Phi Beta Kappa. Besides, I just want to kiss her."

"For how long?"

"Forever. It's a lot of fun. Do you know that?"

"I know."

"Do you ever kiss Lara?"

"No."

"Why not? It's fun."

"It's more complicated than that."

"What's complicated? Just reach over with your lips and kiss."

"It's not physically complicated. I still feel married to my first wife. I'm not ready yet for any kind of deep emotional commitment."

"Then just kiss her and forget about commitments."

"I wish I could."

"If you want, I'll drive us home and you and Lara can sit in the back seat and kiss."

"No, I'll drive."

"Okay—then Julie and I'll sit in the back seat."

"Paul, I'm your home teacher. You're new at this, so I want to give you a few rules my priest adviser gave me a long time ago. The first rule is—you should never be alone in a room with Julie. Okay?"

"How about in an elevator? Is that okay?"

"I guess so. Rule number two is—don't go parking in some secluded spot. That could lead to trouble."

"I agree—it could lead to a lot of trouble."

"You understand what I'm saying then?" I asked hopefully.

"Sure—I don't even own a car. If I stole one to go park with Julie, that'd lead to big trouble."

I sighed, and then continued. "Rule number three—when temptation comes, run two miles a day."

Sudden insight flooded into Paul's mind. "So that's why so many guys jog!"

"Rule number four—when you're tempted, start singing a church hymn and that'll help you through. Okay, will you follow those rules?"

"Sure, they sound easy enough."

"Oh, one other thing—sometimes a cold shower will help."

"You know," Paul reflected as we walked back to the car, "in high school, I could never figure out why my bishop kept warning us about things like this. But it was easy for me. I wasn't dating, and the only girl I liked would've frozen my lips if I'd tried to kiss her."

We put the fish in the ice chest and waited for Julie and Lara.

"Besides," he said, "I had calculus. You know, Sam, calculus should be part of the rules too."

*   *   *   *   *   *

We drove to town and dropped Julie off at her dorm and Paul at his aunt's house.

A few minutes later I pulled in front of Lara's house and parked. After watching Julie and Paul kiss outside the dorm a few minutes before, I was in the mood for romance.

"Did you give the fish to Paul?" Lara asked.

"Sure—why?"

"It still smells fishy around here."

Inconspicuously I sniffed my hands and realized I was the source of the smell. I casually dangled my left hand out the car window and buried my right hand in my pants pocket. It looked a little ridiculous.

"You know," I said with a grin, "I was talking to Paul today about the dangers of kissing too much and how it can lead to other things. He asked if I'd ever kissed you. He said I should try it. I told him it was more complicated than that, but he said it wasn't complicated—that you just reach over with your lips and kiss. Isn't that funny?"

"Oh yes," she said, laughing more than I would have preferred.

"I told him it's taken me time to adjust to losing Charly. That's why I haven't even tried—up to now, I mean."

I slid closer to her, my left hand sticking out the window.

"And I respect you for that, too," she said. "I think it's best for a couple to become good friends first."

"Lara, I consider you a good friend—a very good friend."

I couldn't slide any closer and still have my left hand out the window in the breeze, so I just leaned toward her. She looked strangely at my position. I must have looked like a monkey at a zoo.

Never mind the smell, I thought, I need arms for this. I'm going to kiss her tonight. How long it's been since I felt this way! Wow, her face is nice. And her neck—I must kiss her neck.

"Lara," I said, sliding next to her, "lately I've thought about holding you close and kissing you."

"I've thought about that too," she said.

Terrific! I thought.

"But we both have very high standards, don't we?"

"Standards? What have standards got to do with it? I'm talking about your basic goodnight kiss."

"We're not going to give in to the temptation to kiss, are we?"

"We aren't?"

"You know," she continued cheerfully, "when I was just a young girl, I decided to save my kisses for the man I was going to marry. And I think maybe you've set those same high standards too, haven't you?"

She smiled warmly at me, while I stared at her in shock.

"You got to be kidding!"

"Sam?" she asked, sensing something very wrong.

"You won't even kiss me unless I agree to marry you?"

"Sam!"

"Lara, so help me, I've tried. I've overlooked your weird eating habits. Why can't you eat sugar? I think it's stupid not to eat sugar! Sugar is as American as—as apple pie! And I've tried to ignore your photographic memory. But this—not kissing! Do you know how many dates we've had? Okay, at first I wasn't ready to kiss—but now I am. For crying out loud, who can put up with all your nonsense? You're just driving me away, you know that? I've really tried. But this time you've gone too far!"

I jumped out of the car, slammed the door, escorted her to the porch, and escaped as fast as I could.

Chapter Ten

"Lara, this is silly. Why wouldn't you let me apologize on the phone? Why'd we have to come here?"

"Because this is where we started."

"All right, but did you clear using the room?"

"Of course. You go first—careful, don't bump your head."

I crawled under the high council table and she followed, dragging a picnic basket after her.

"What's in the basket?"

"Later. First of all, you've got a lot of explaining to do about what you've been doing."

"It's only been a week."

"But a busy week for you!" she accused. "Sam, how do you think I felt when people told me about the things you were doing? For a while I was getting a phone call every fifteen minutes. I thought you'd gone berserk."

"Who told you?"

"Relatives, friends, single adults. I wrote it all down. Shall we go through it now?"

"I don't see how that will—"

"Sam, we're going through this!" she said coolly as she opened a small notebook. "Let's see," she said, reading from her notes, "you called up the Deseret Gym and asked for a list of single women who play racquetball. How many did you take out?"

"Just one."

"And?"

"She beat me—terrific backhand."

"So?"

"I never want to see her again in my life."

She glanced at her notebook. "Here's one I find difficult to believe. You hung around an LDS bookstore watching girls who buy books about temple marriage."

"I needed something to do during my lunch hours."

"Let's see," she said, flipping to another page. "You took out all five check-out girls at a Safeway store. Is that right?"

"Well, not all at once, of course."

"This next one really surprises me. You took out a girl who's still in high school."

"I did?"

"To refresh your memory of the details, she was the one who worked at McDonald's."

"It wasn't a date—she's taking her driver's exam next week and she wanted practice driving a car with a manual shift. Her father came with us."

"I can't read my writing on the next one. It looks like 'ground beef girl.'"

"She puts it into the little plastic boxes and seals it."

"You mean another one from Safeway?"

"Well, you know their motto, 'Since we're neighbors, let's be friends.'"

"How did Hamburger Patty work out?"

"I made the mistake of asking about her goals. She said someday she hopes she can move up to steaks."

"Is that all you dated?"

"Well, there was a women's stake softball tournament."

"You dated one of the players?"

"Sort of," I said vaguely.

"More? You mean the entire team?"

"I took them out for banana splits and told stories about my mission. They all said it was more inspiring than the Old Testament."

"Why'd you even bother to call me last night? I mean, there were still hardware stores, banks, drugstores, li-

95

braries. Why bother to get back to me?"

"After all the others, I finally decided . . . I'm not sure, but it's entirely possible that I may be falling in love with you."

"It is?"

"Indications point that way at the present time."

"When will you be sure?"

"I don't know."

"But indications actually are pointing? Good grief, Sam, this sounds like a weather report. You're saying you might be in love with me?"

"You've got it, Ace. I'm as surpised as you are."

"Why?"

"Remember the first time we were under this table. It was such a crazy night—for a split second I thought you were Charly. She was always doing wild things, and I'd never been under the table with a girl before."

"Me neither."

"But one thing's sure—you're not Charly. So why am I falling in love with you?"

"That's a good question, but I've got a better one. Why'd it take three busloads of girls to figure that out?"

"I tried the others—on a high moral plain, you understand—but I came back to you. Why's that so hard to understand? They do it all the time on TV with deodorants."

"Talk slower, Sam," she said, writing in her notebook. "I want to get this all down for my journal."

"Okay, so I ran away and dated a couple of dozen girls last week. There was another reason. You have one drawback."

"Just one?"

"You're overqualified—too smart, too spiritual, too much initiative. For all I know, you make more money than I do. Last week, when I was still mad at you, I pictured us married and people coming up to us, slapping you on the back, and asking, 'How's the little man?'"

"Okay, I agree—I'm a monster."

"Cute though."

"Oh, thanks! Last week I decided most of all I wanted to be cute. You know, it hasn't been an easy week for me either. I kept asking myself, where did I go wrong? I finally decided it was when my bishop interviewed me about goals when I was twelve years old. He told me I could achieve anything I put my mind to, and I believed him. He was right, but he didn't tell me that if I was too successful I'd scare all the boys away. You're not the first, you know. In my senior year in college, I was solely responsible for ten freshmen girls getting married. A guy'd start to date me, get intimidated, and run out and propose to the first eighteen-year-old girl he met."

She opened the picnic basket and pulled out a book and gave it to me.

"What's this for?"

"We need to improve our communications. This book talks about active listening. Let's try one of his examples. Suppose you were my son and you were taking piano lessons. You come home from a lesson and say you don't want to go anymore."

A pause.

"Well?"

"Go ahead and say it."

"I don't want to take piano anymore."

"Not like that—say it like you mean it."

"*I'm not taking any more dumb lessons!*"

"You're mad at the teacher, aren't you."

A long pause.

"Well, aren't you?"

"Lara, how should I know? It's your example."

"Pretend the teacher really cuts you down."

"I hate the teacher!"

"You don't like to go there every week, do you?"

"No, she's always putting me down! I can never please her!"

"You'd like to quit the whole thing, wouldn't you?"

"Yeah and I will too! So don't try to stop me! And there's another thing. *Quit trying to make me eat spinach!*"

We both stopped and looked at each other.

"Spinach?" she asked.

"I'm sorry. I don't know how that got out."

"Hello there."

We looked out and saw the stake president's shoes. We crawled out from under the table, both of us blushing.

"I suppose you're wondering why we were under the high council table with a picnic basket talking about piano lessons," I said.

"Yes, but I'm not going to ask. Whatever it is, it's a ward problem. Good night."

He stopped halfway to the door and turned back with a grin. "I know what you mean. I didn't like piano lessons either."

*　　　*　　　*　　　*　　　*　　　*

The next day after work, Lara and I helped my folks pick cucumbers for pickles. My parents were inside getting the jars and lids ready.

Paul and Julie showed up.

"Ta da!" Julie shouted. "Here we are, the stars of physics research! Paul took me to his lab and made me a diamond."

"Actually," Paul modestly explained, "it's just a microscopic diamond."

"Have you two had dinner?" I asked.

"I don't remember," Paul grinned. "Julie, have we eaten?"

She giggled. "After you gave me that tiny diamond and proposed, I can't remember anything else."

"Proposed?" I asked. "Proposed what?"

"Marriage," Paul answered. "We're going to get married—to each other."

We had created a monster.

"When?" Lara asked, as stunned as I was.

"Any time we want."

"We need a license and a blood test," Paul said happily.

"Do I pass the test? I have blood."

"I know," Paul blushed. "That's what makes you so warm. Hey, how about next Saturday?"

"Okay—I always wanted to get married on a Saturday. Paul, can we stay up and watch 'Saturday Night Live'?"

"Julie," he blushed, "we'll *be* 'Saturday Night Live.' "

"You can't get married just like that!" I growled.

"Julie," Lara explained, "you've got to pick out a wedding dress, then there are invitations, and a reception to be planned. It takes weeks to get everything planned."

"Sure—that's what you do if your parents are around, but ours aren't. They won't be back in the states for another six months. Besides, we don't want all the expense. We'll rent a wedding dress at the temple. The most important thing is to be married in the temple."

"Julie, you'd better talk to your bishop about this," I grumbled.

"We did," Paul said.

"What'd he say?"

"Congratulations."

"You've only known each other for a few weeks," I said. "Take more time."

Paul looked at his watch and observed the second hand. "That's thirty seconds. I still feel the same way. How about you, Julie?"

"I waited for you," she teased. "Why didn't you ever write?"

"C'mon Paul, what do you really know about girls? How many girls have you ever dated? I mean, besides the girl with the frozen hand and the other, the one with bugs."

"That's a story I'd love to hear," Lara said.

"What does it matter how many others I've dated?" Paul argued. "I'm twenty-four. This isn't exactly a teenage wedding." Then remembering Julie, he asked, "Is it?"

"No, but just barely."

"Don't rush into this."

"Why are you both against us getting married?" Julie asked.

Lara turned to me. "Why are we?"

"It's obvious, isn't it? Julie is too—well, alive for Paul. I always pictured him marrying someone like Madame Curie. She'd stand by him in the lab."

"Sure," Lara added. "And Julie'd marry a PE major and they'd do morning calisthenics together."

"That's why we object," I said. "You're both so different from each other."

"I know we are," Paul said, "but it works for us. Julie's the most wonderful thing that's ever happened to me. All of a sudden the world is full of colors I never even knew existed."

"And Paul is the nicest and smartest guy I've ever known," Julie said. "Do you know he has nearly all the hymns memorized?"

"Paul," I suggested, "what'd be wrong with waiting six months to see if you still love each other then?"

"No! I'm tired of singing and jogging! I've taken so many cold showers this week, I think I've got diaper rash."

"And I'm tired of riding elevators," Julie complained.

"Elevators?" I asked.

"Paul said it was okay."

"I want to get married!" Paul called out.

"That's not a good enough reason," I said.

Lara turned to me. "What exactly do you want to happen first?"

"Marriage is a big step, Lara," I said.

"I understand that, Sam.

"What do you want?" she asked. "A letter from the First Presidency saying it's all right? If they get along, if they love each other, if they can go to the temple, why on earth shouldn't they get married?"

100

Now they were all looking at me.

"It's a big step," I repeated.

"We're ready for it," Julie said.

"Sometimes married life is tough."

"We'll face whatever comes," Paul said.

I shrugged my shoulders. "Okay. Congratulations, you two."

By way of advice, I started the story of the two frogs, but Julie turned the hose on me, and Lara joined her. Then Paul joined me and we started a mammoth water fight.

Later that day Paul asked me if, after the ceremony, I would drive him and Julie to the motel he had reserved for their honeymoon.

"I could take a taxi," he said, blushing a little, "but I'd be too embarrassed. I'd tell him to take us to a motel —and he'd suspect something."

*   *   *   *   *   *

Lara and I watched as Paul and Julie knelt at an altar in the temple.

The temple president counseled them. "You know, only in one of these temples can you be married for time and eternity. It's not because these buildings are more beautiful nor because we think we're any better than anybody else. It's because the prophet Elijah as an angel returned to earth and brought back the sealing power of the priesthood. And that's why you're here today—because of Elijah."

Lara was watching Julie and Paul, and I was watching Lara. It was so comfortable to be sitting next to her in the temple.

"Now you both want this marriage to last into the eternities, don't you?"

They both nervously nodded yes.

"Well, if it's going to last that long, then it has to last

today, doesn't it? You'll never reach forever if you don't reach five years, or ten or fifty. And that means you have to work at it day by day, because eternity is made of days, and each day is important and carries the thread of eternity."

I reached over and held Lara's hand. She looked at me and smiled.

"We're taught that the home is to be led by the priesthood. Young man, do you know how you are to rule over your wife?"

Paul was too nervous to remember his name, so he just smiled.

"The key is found in the Doctrine and Covenants. Does anybody here know the section that talks about how the priesthood functions."

"Section 121," Lara said.

"That's right. It says that no power or influence can or ought to be maintained by the priesthood except with gentleness and meekness and unconditional love. And that's how a husband should treat his wife."

Paul nodded.

"The pattern the Lord has set up is the husband follows the Savior and his teachings, and the wife follows her husband. Young man, you love your wife as much as the Savior loves the Church, and you'll be blessed in your marriage."

Then he performed the ceremony for time and all eternity.

Afterwards we treated them to lunch, drove them to their motel, and waved goodbye.

That night I took Lara to supper at a Mexican restaurant.

"It was nice to be in the temple with you today," I said as we waited for our food. "You're beautiful in white."

"Just in white?" she teased.

"No, in anything."

"Lately I've been winning some clothes at the store. Steve has a contest every month for the one who sells the most. I won this dress."

"Is Steve married?" I asked, a little jealous.

"Yes—for now he is, but his marriage is on the rocks. He works too hard, and he's never home. By the way, he said he'd like to meet you. Why don't you pick me up after work Monday?"

"Okay."

Our salads came.

I looked at my watch. "Well, Paul and Julie have been married now for five hours."

She looked at me, smiled a little, and glanced at her watch. "Yes, that's about right."

"I suppose they're having dinner now."

She blushed. "Yes, this is dinner time, all right."

"And tomorrow morning, they'll have breakfast together, won't they."

She laughed. "I'm sure they will, because tomorrow morning it'll be breakfast time. Sam, before you embarrass me, can we change the subject?"

"Okay—your choice."

"I'm in my ward choir and we're singing tomorrow. Want to come hear us?"

"Are you any good?"

"No, but we're enthusiastic. Our bishop says we're great."

"Bishops always say that. Just once I'd like to hear one say, 'We'd like to thank our ward choir. They are adequate, aren't they. We don't have much musical talent in our ward, as must be obvious by now. The way the choir sounded today is just about what we expected. Thank you, choir, for your slightly amusing rendition of a favorite hymn."

"Sam, you've got a mean streak a mile wide," she joked.

The waitress brought our food.

"Oh, look at that!" she said. "I love Mexican food!" She took a bite of her taco. "Oh, that's good!"

I watched her enjoy the food. She was beautiful even when chewing.

"Why aren't you eating?" she asked.

"Lara, I love you."

"Really?" she asked, putting down the taco. "You mean indications have finally pointed to love?"

"They have."

"That makes me very happy." She picked up her taco and took another bite. I just sat and watched her.

"Isn't your enchilada going to get cold?" she asked.

"I don't care. Lara, I want to hold your hand."

"You do?" she asked, her taco stopping midway to her mouth.

"Yes."

Pause.

"If you hold my hand, I won't be able to finish my taco."

"I'm sorry about the timing."

She sighed. "The greatest tribute I can give you is that a returned missionary from New Mexico is now laying down her taco. Look, you may as well hold both hands—I'm not doing anything with the other."

"I love you very much."

"You know what?" she asked. "Right offhand, I'd bet we're going to kiss tonight, aren't we."

"I wouldn't be surprised."

"I don't want you to think this'll require any permanent commitment, but it will mean we love each other, won't it?"

"Yes, that's what it'll mean," I said.

"I can hardly wait."

"I guess we should finish our food," I said.

"Sam, look away. I don't want you to see this. I'm about to set a world record in taco snarfing."

We ate quickly without much talk.

After paying the bill, we jumped in the car and left. I raced to a place I used to go in high school after dates. It was a vacant lot then—now it was a housing development. Then I decided to see if my car would go where I used to go when I had my jeep. We got stuck in a ditch and had to phone a wrecker service.

Three hours later I pulled outside her house, turned

off the ignition, turned on the radio, reached over with my lips, and kissed her.

A few seconds later, we decided to breathe.

"Wow!" I gasped.

"It was adequate?" she teased.

"Much more than adequate."

"For me too. I think having the radio on to 'Mystery Theater' was a nice touch."

"Thanks."

"It really set the stage."

I held her and together we tried to figure out who killed the butler.

"Did you have the onions or did I?" she asked.

"I did—sorry."

"I can take onion breath—I've been to New Mexico."

All that night, after I'd gone home, I had heartburn.

*　　　*　　　*　　　*　　　*　　　*

Monday after work I dropped by the store where Lara worked and met Steve. He was about my age, enthusiastic and charming.

"So you're Sam. Lara's told me a lot about you. As far as I see it, you're the only one standing in the way of her becoming a very rich lady."

"How's that?"

"Running off with her every Saturday cuts into her sales."

"She tells me she's doing better than anyone else."

"She is, but think what she could do if she worked Saturdays. Why don't you let her do that, and I'll give you both five percent of what I make from her sales that day."

"I'd rather have her with me."

"She's a wonder—I hope you know that. For our best customers she's memorized names, faces, dress measurements, color preferences. When we get a new shipment, she goes through it, picks out the ones they'd like, calls them up, and they come down and buy. People are calling on the phone to make appointments with her. I've never seen anything like it. She could be a very rich woman in a few years. I just hope I can keep her happy enough here so she won't start her own store. She'd be my toughest competition. By the way, Lara, why don't you pick out another dress—you won last month's contest."

Lara walked over to a dress rack.

"And what do you do, Sam?"

"I work at the computer center at the U."

"Is there any money in that?"

"Not much—working for the state, you know."

"You going to do that your whole life?"

"I haven't decided."

"When are you going to decide?"

"I don't know."

"Let me give you some advice. Don't sit on your dreams. Think big and act big. You can be an eagle in this world, or you can be a cow."

A secretary told him there was a call waiting.

"Do you know what that's for?" he asked. "I'm working on a deal to build four new stores in this area. In five years, I'll be rich enough so I'll never have to work again if I don't want to. Be an eagle, Sam."

The next day at work, as someone shoved a fouled-up program over my desk for the thousandth time, I had an almost uncontrollable urge to moo.

Chapter Eleven

We were kneading bread together. "My parents'd like to meet you," she said.

"Oh?"

"Relax, it's no big deal. I've told them so much about you and Adam, they just want to get acquainted. They said if you can take me up some weekend, they'll show Adam the horses and cows and chickens. He'd love that, wouldn't he?"

Friday after work we drove to her home, a farm near Idaho Falls. A few handshakes and "How was the trip?" and Adam and I were safely tucked away in our room for the night.

The next morning I stayed in the room as long as possible before going downstairs. Finally Adam and I walked into the kitchen, where the family waited for us.

Adam quietly and efficiently consumed everything they put in front of him for breakfast but didn't say much. After breakfast he got out of his high chair and sat on Lara's lap.

Lara's older brother Bob and his wife, Faye, were there plus their four children. When he found out I worked with computers, his eyes lit up. "Computers, hey? I've got a problem for you. If a chicken and a half can lay an egg and a half in a day and a half, how many eggs does one chicken lay in one day?"

"One," I said confidently, still eating.

"Nope," he chuckled. "That's what everyone says, but it's not right."

My face began to redden. "I'm sure it's one."

"Dead wrong," he grinned. "Hey, Lara, I gave your computer man a problem he can't work. I thought you said he was smart."

I asked for a piece of paper and a pencil. As the conversation swirled around me, I worked on the problem, getting madder every minute and less able to think clearly.

Every few minutes Bob would grin and ask, "Got it yet?"

Large drops of sweat cascaded down my back.

The dishes were cleared. Bob went outside with his father. They took Adam with them but I stayed hunched over my paper.

Lara breezed by with a load of stacked dishes and whispered, "It doesn't matter, Sam."

"I'll figure it out."

After the dishes were done, Lara came back, kissed me, and whispered, "Two-thirds."

"What?" I snapped.

"The answer is two-thirds."

"How do you know?"

"It's a problem my father gave us when we were little."

"You didn't have to tell me," I complained. "I would've worked it out by myself."

"Sorry—I just wanted to help. Well, I have to take a shower. See you later."

In a few minutes, Bob and his father brought Adam in the house. He had just had his first horseback ride.

"Got that problem yet?" Bob asked.

"Two-thirds," I said.

"Right—did Lara tell you?"

"Yes."

"I thought so. Well here's another problem you might like . . ."

In the afternoon the larger family came—more

brothers and sisters and their children. I stood, smiled, shook hands, and forgot their names.

There was always the unspoken question on their faces about Lara and me—were we engaged yet, and if we weren't, when would we be? And if we weren't going to get engaged, why had she brought me home?

Lara was one of three daughters and four brothers. She was the second daughter, but the only one not married. The youngest girl had married a few months before.

After lunch Bob brought the question out in the open. "Hey, Sis, have you and Sam got anything to tell us?"

"About what, Bob?"

"Are you going to get married?"

Bob's wife tried to shush him, but that was impossible. I was glowing red.

"We don't know, Bob," Lara said.

"You'd better get something going soon—you're not getting any younger, you know."

"Thanks for the reminder, Bob," she said, more politely than I would have.

I looked at Lara. With all the crawling, nursing, wetting, walking babies in the room, with all the husbands and wives, you could cut the pressure she felt with a knife.

As soon as I could leave without too much notice, I took Adam upstairs to give him a bath—any excuse to escape. While he played in the tub, I looked out the window and wished we'd never come.

A few minutes later, I heard Lara at the door. While I'd been rearranging my thoughts, Adam had managed to open the shampoo bottle. The whole tub was full of suds. His head looked like the cherry on a pile of whipped cream.

"Sam?" she asked.

"Yes."

"I want to take Adam to see the horses again. Will you be long?"

"Not very long."

"Is everything okay?"

"Fine—I'm giving him a bath."

"Can I help?"

I opened the door. She rushed into my arms.

"I'm sorry, Sam. Don't let them bug you, okay?"

We kissed. Adam looked over at us and laughed.

"Daddy kissing," he chuckled.

"Don't knock it, kid," I said.

Lara viewed the white tornado. "Think you have enough soap?"

"I'm willing to share." I scooped up a bunch of bubbles and plopped them on her head.

She just looked at me.

I had Adam stand up, ran water to rinse him off, lifted him out of the tub, then turned quickly and set Lara screaming into the water.

We retreated to our room and I got Adam dressed. A few minutes later we stepped gingerly outside, looking for Lara, but she was nowhere to be seen. We went to the barn and talked with Bob.

Lara's father took Adam on another horseback ride.

A few minutes later, Bob and I were leaning against a fence looking at the horses. Lara came out with a bucket.

"What's in the bucket?" Bob asked.

"Water—I'm going to throw it on Sam. Move away."

"No, she's not," I assured him. "It's an old clown routine. The bucket is full of confetti and she makes us think it's full of water. She's done that routine dozens of times at ward parties in Utah. Don't worry, Bob."

"Bob, it's really full of water. Move away from Sam."

"Bob," I countered, "you've known Lara far longer than I have. She's not the type who'd walk up and throw water on a houseguest, is she? I mean, she's a very conscientious person. So don't worry. It's just a clown routine."

Bob relaxed.

Lara chucked the contents of the bucket at us. We both yelled as the water drenched us.

"Sam," she said calmly, "in some ways I've changed being around you." Then she walked back to the house.

"Isn't she terrific?" I roared with laughter, slapping Bob on his soggy shoulders.

*   *   *   *   *   *

That night the whole family got together for one giant family home evening. We had thirty children in the house along with their parents.

We were just finishing up when another family arrived—a tall, rugged man, his blonde wife, and their two children.

Lara rushed into the hall and hugged them both. She knelt down to adore the one-year-old boy, then stood up to fuss over the babe in arms.

"Do you know who they are?" Bob asked me.

"No."

"Hasn't Lara ever told you about Craig? She nearly married him before her mission."

Lara brought them into the congested living room and introduced them to me.

"Ann, you look so good!" Lara said. "How do you keep up with two little children?"

"Well, it keeps me busy, I'll tell you," Ann smiled happily. "But I love it—except for the two A.M. feedings, that is."

"Oh, look at these darling children!" Lara's mother bubbled, coming in from the kitchen. "They are so precious, Craig."

"Lara, do you want to hold our baby?" Ann asked.

"Do I!" She lovingly picked up the baby and held her. "Look, she's smiling at me! Oh, she's so sweet."

"Probably just gas pains," Bob said.

Just then the phone rang. The only reason I know is that I was sitting next to it. Otherwise nobody would have heard it over the noise.

Lara's father answered it. "Lara, it's a person-to-person long distance call for you."

The room quieted down as parents warned children to be quiet. This was a house where person-to-person long distance calls meant either great happiness or severe tragedy.

Lara, still holding Ann's baby, answered it. "Hello. Oh, Steve, it's you. . . . You got the loan for the other stores? That's fantastic! . . . When do they start construction? . . . That soon? Oh, you must be excited. . . . Do you think I could do that? . . . Well, at least one of us is confident, because I'm not. Look, can I let you know next week? . . . Well, okay, call me tomorrow and I'll see if I've decided by then. . . . Thanks, Steve. Goodbye."

She hung up and everyone waited.

"What was that all about?" Bob asked.

"My boss called to tell me he's got the money to build four more stores. He asked me to be an assistant manager where I work now, and to take over most of the details, because he's not going to have time to worry about it now."

Lara handed the baby back to Ann.

"Is it a lot more money?" Bob asked.

"Yes, quite a bit more."

"Take it! Hey, I bet you'll be making more than Sam, won't you?"

"The money's not important," she said.

"Boy, I can tell you're not raising a family," Ann joked.

"If you two ever decide to get married," Bob continued, "why don't you have Sam stay home with the children and you keep working?" Bob laughed. "No kidding, I read somewhere that some kooky couple is doing just that."

I looked at Lara's parents—they were discouraged. More than anything, they wanted her married and a mother, not a business executive. But because they loved her, they tried to be supportive. "Lara," her father said, putting his arm around her, "if that's what you really want, then more power to you."

"You've always worked hard, haven't you?" her mother added.

"I always knew Lara'd do good," Craig said, at the same time reaching out to hold his wife's hand.

She sat down beside me and we quietly endured the rest of the evening.

At eleven-thirty, tucked away in my room, I lay awake thinking. Finally, hoping a breeze would put me to sleep, I opened my window. I could hear someone crying. It was Lara in the next room. Her window was open too.

I undid my screen enough to be able to look out. "Lara?" I called softly.

"Sam?"

"Undo the latches so I can see you." In a minute we were talking to each other out our windows.

"Are you okay?" I asked.

"Yes. I'm sorry for crying so loud."

"Is it because you still love Craig?" I asked painfully.

"No, it's nothing like that. It's just coming home. I'm such a misfit here, such a failure. And it gets worse every year. Why do they make me feel so rotten?"

"They don't mean to."

"I nearly cried watching my mother fuss over Craig's kids. She wishes I'd married him, because then all of us'd be together in this valley. I'm the only one who's left, and the only one still single."

"You have to live your own life."

"I know. What shall I do about Steve's offer?"

"Don't do anything. I don't trust us here. Let's both make a no-decision pact. I won't ask you to marry me this weekend, and you won't give Steve an answer. Your relatives want us to wrap it up this weekend. But we've got to fight it. Don't let them psych you out, no matter how many kids they parade past you. If we're going to get married, let's make the decision on our terms, in our own world—in my car listening to 'Mystery Theater.'"

"Thanks," she sighed. By stretching out, we could just manage to hold hands. "Sam, I think you're wonderful."

"You got good judgment, kid."

*   *   *   *   *   *

The next day was Sunday and we went to church. The high council speaker talked about the importance of the family. He quoted a statement by Brigham Young that any young man over twenty-five who isn't married is a menace to the community.

Lara snickered and punched me in the side.

He commented on the ever-increasing number of couples living together without marriage. He quoted a statistic claiming that only thirteen percent of families in the country consist of a husband, a wife who stays home, and children. He warned about women who believe they must leave the home to work.

Sunday afternoon after supper, we took a little walk.

"Lara, married people don't understand the pressure we feel when they talk about families. What's it like for a woman over twenty-five with no prospects for marriage? What's it like when she goes to church? She'd get married if she could, but nobody's come along. What does she do?"

"She copes, Sam. She gets hobbies, she works hard in her job, she gives help to others. Sometimes she does what I did last night—she cries."

"Why don't people who speak about eternal families ever say that those who don't have that opportunity but remain faithful will not be shorted any blessings in the hereafter?"

"They don't say it because they're married," she said.

Sunday evening Steve called. True to our pact, Lara gave him only a maybe.

114

On Monday we were both glad to leave. An hour down the road I asked her to tell me about Craig.

"We started going together during our senior year in high school. The next fall he went on a mission and I went to college. Two years later he returned. I wanted him to get a college education, but he wanted to stay home and take over his dad's place. I loved school too much, and he loved farming. We still cared about each other, but we broke up. I guess I outgrew him."

I cringed. "Think you'll ever outgrow me, Lara?"

"No, Sam, I won't."

"But look how you're moving up. How much did Steve offer you?"

"What does it matter? I don't care about the money. Sam, I love you."

"Why, Lara? I'm a second-string computer programmer in a dead-end job. If I don't progress any further than this, then I'm a failure—pure and simple."

"So you feel threatened by my success."

"Don't tell me how I feel. They're my feelings, not yours. I'm the only one who can say how I feel."

She sighed. "Okay—how do you feel?"

"I don't know."

She smiled. "Well, that was certainly enlightening, wasn't it."

"I love you. And someday I'm going to ask you to marry me."

"Which someday, Sam?"

"The problem isn't how I feel about you. The problem is how I feel about myself."

"I don't care if you sell apples on the street—I'll still love you."

"I imagine us playing checkers in our old age and you deliberately losing just to keep me happy. That's not right."

"And it's not right for you to think you always have to win at checkers either, is it?"

"No, I guess not."

"Okay, Sam, I'll lay it on the line. Nothing else much matters to me anymore except you and Adam. If you want me to be scatterbrained, I'll do it. I'll burn your food, I'll wrinkle your clothes, and I'll lose a sock from each pair. I'll overdraw your checking account. Just tell me what you want from a wife and I'll do it."

"I appreciate that, but no, you be the best Lara you can be."

"Oh Sam," she moaned, "not that."

An hour later we pulled into a grocery store and gas station in a small town.

"Do you want a snack?" I asked as we went inside to pay for the gas.

"Whatever you think," she said blandly.

"Well, would you like an apple?"

"You decide, Sam. I can't make up my mind."

"I know you like apples—shall I get you one?"

"It's so hard for me to decide."

"Lara, I know you're practicing being a helpless female, but I need to know if you want an apple."

"You know best, Sam."

I went to the back of the store and got an apple. When I returned, she was grinning at me triumphantly.

"I want a Hostess Twinkie."

"No—it has white refined sugar in it."

"That's what I want. Please buy me one."

"I know what you're trying to do, but I'm not going to let you do it."

The lady behind the counter glanced up from her magazine to watch us.

"It'd be the best thing for us, Sam."

She had a package in her hand, but I managed to pull it away from her. "You must really love me even to consider doing this."

"Sam," she said seriously, "give me the Twinkie."

"And what about your teeth—don't you owe them any consideration?"

She grabbed another package from the shelf and dramatically tore open the wrapper. Before taking a bite, she hesitated and started to read the ingredients.

"Sugar . . ."

"Lara, you don't have to do this for me."

" . . . enriched white flour, corn syrup, dextrose, mono and diglycerides, sodium caseinate, polysorbate 60 . . . "

I wrestled it from her, squishing the filling all over my hand.

"Hey, you two, take it easy!" the lady warned us.

"You can't stop me, Sam." She picked up another package, ripped it open, and took a large bite out of the Twinkie.

"Lara," I said slowly, "that was as noble a thing as I've ever seen. Words cannot tell how I feel now."

"Seventy cents for the two," the lady said, "the one you have all over your hand and the one she's eating."

"Hey, Sam, these are really good! Let's get one for Adam too."

"What have I done?" I moaned.

"You've bought three Twinkies, that's what you've done," the lady said.

"Lara, show this lady your teeth."

"Not now—they're full of cake."

"A dollar five—you might as well lick it off your hand because you're paying for it."

"Lady, what's the name of this store?" I asked. "I'm putting this in my journal."

Chapter Twelve

It was billed as a confidence-building survival experience for business executives. Steve told Lara about it at work the day after our return from Idaho when she talked to him about me. He phoned the office in California and they booked us for the Southern Utah site for the next week.

"Three hundred dollars?" I moaned when she told me how much it was going to cost.

"Think of it as tuition."

We drove down the next Thursday. The camp consisted of several tents and a couple of jeeps in a rocky ravine. We met the head of the program, a tall, lean man named Brock.

"Do you know who comes here?" he asked. "Failures come here. Oh sure, they may be pulling down a hundred thousand a year, but they're still failures. Do you know why they're failures? Because they don't have Self-Knowledge. And do you know what we do with them? We turn them into men who can match these mountains. And then they have Self-Knowledge."

As we left him, I told Lara I was sure they'd turn her into a woman who could match the mountains. I didn't want her to worry.

The first thing I noticed about the training was that they starved us. Wild turnips and jerky have never been among my favorite foods.

After sleeping in a tent with a wheezing, snoring business executive from Chicago, I faced breakfast—jerky, raisins, bread, and water.

Then we took a hike with Brock. After a few minutes, Lara and I figured out what he was doing. He would hike a fast pace until he was about five minutes ahead of the slowest members of the group, then sit down and rest until they just caught up with us. Then he'd take off again, giving the impression he was superhuman in endurance.

We raced with him, and by doing so, were able to get the longest rests.

The next day we were scheduled for another hike, this time without Brock to lead us. A man named Talby took over the leadership of the group from the start. He was a corporation executive and was used to taking charge.

We reached our destination, a large jutting rock, easily visible from camp, a distance of about ten miles.

About three in the afternoon, we started back to camp. The route back was more difficult—we had no landmark to follow. About an hour underway, we came to a bend where two canyons forked out.

"This way," Talby said. "We take the right fork."

"No," Lara corrected. "We go left."

Talby said he knew he was right.

"Lara, are you sure?" I asked.

"Every time we came to a fork, I looked for a landmark and used a memory gimmick to help me remember. I'm sure. We have to go left."

"If she says we should go left, then we'd better go left."

"Are you going to believe a woman instead of me?" he challenged.

"I'm going to believe this woman."

The rest decided Talby was right.

"What kind of a man are you—letting a woman lead you around by the nose?"

"She doesn't make mistakes about things like this."

119

They all started off. Talby turned to yell at us. "Brock's not going to be happy about having to come out here and rescue you!" They disappeared around the bend.

"Sam, what if I'm wrong?" she asked.

"Are you?"

She turned back to check her landmarks. "No, I'm right."

"Then let's go."

In three more hours we were back in camp. Then we drove around in jeeps for an hour before we found Talby and the others.

Lara and I couldn't face much more jerky, so we both ate light.

That night Brock made an announcement. "I hope you all ate enough for supper, because tomorrow is your main survival test. At four in the morning we'll be taking each of you into a separate remote area. All you'll have is a flint, a jackknife, and a canteen of water. What you eat will be what you're smart enough to find. You'll be on your own, but we'll have observers posted watching you so you won't kill yourself. And do you know what this will do for you?"

"Wipe us out," Lara whispered.

"It'll give you Self-Knowledge."

Lara and I asked if we could be together for the test.

The next morning they got us up while it was still dark, and drove each of us to separate areas. The morning brought a lot of heat and no food. Where were the berries, where were the fish, where was the water, where were the wild onions?

*   *   *   *   *   *

It was afternoon and the canyon walls were ovens. Lara and I sat in the shade of a large boulder and sweat. We hadn't talked for over half an hour.

120

"How you doing?" I finally asked.

She cleared her throat. "Sam," she rasped, "even my throat is sunburned."

I went to great effort to turn my head to look at her face.

"Your nose too," I said.

"Before they have the viewing, have the funeral director put makeup on my face. If you make it through, promise me you'll tell him that."

A few minutes later I continued our conversation. "We're going to make it through. Do you know why?"

"No, why?"

"Because between the two of us, we paid six hundred dollars to come out here and have somebody starve us. We're going to survive, and when we get back, we're going to warn people to stay away. That's why we're going to make it."

"No, we're going to starve."

"No, we're not. We're going to get up and kill a very large animal and eat its flesh."

She chuckled. "What animal is going to let us do that?"

"We'll use cunning and stealth."

"Sam, the smart quick animals kill the weak ones. It's the law of the jungle. Now only the smart ones are left. The dumb, clumsy ones have already been eaten. There's no hope for us."

I reached down and found a small pebble and put it in my mouth.

"What did you do that for?"

"When you're thirsty, put a pebble in your mouth, and your thirst will go away."

She looked at me, shook her head, and chortled to herself.

"There're coyotes around here. Do you know what that means?"

"What?"

"That means there are rabbits around. We will kill a rabbit and eat it."

"How do we kill a rabbit?"

"We set a rabbit trap and lure it with some food."

We were both looking at the opposite boulder as if it were a TV set.

"There's no lettuce here—how do we lure a rabbit?"

My shoulders slumped. "We'll think of something."

"Let's just give up, Sam. It was us against the desert—the desert won."

"I'm not giving up. I paid three hundred dollars and I'm not leaving till I've had at least as much meat as they put on a Big Mac."

"You're going to eat raw meat?" she asked.

"No, I'm going to cook it, using flint and steel to start a fire. C'mon, let's go to work."

"First give me a drink of water."

"We don't have much. You should put a pebble in your mouth."

"Sam, please? Just a little sip."

"Okay." Instead of a tiny sip, she grabbed the canteen with both hands and gulped the water down. I pulled it away.

"Oh, that was good!"

"You said just a sip."

"I'm sorry. Out here I don't seem to have any self-control, or courage, or confidence. Can we sit for a few minutes more?"

"We need to look for food."

"Let me just ask you one question. I've been thinking about it all day."

"Okay."

"When it's so hot out, why doesn't the wax in our ears run out?"

We walked up the canyon. A few minutes later I saw a small rabbit hopping along several feet from us.

"Look!" I whispered.

"Oh, isn't it cute?" she said. "Once I had a bunny rabbit named Fluffy Toes."

"I'm going to kill it and eat its flesh."

"Good—I'll help you."

122

We stalked the rabbit. I found a piece of wood to use for a club. Suddenly I ran toward it, swinging my club. It scurried into a pile of rocks.

"Sam, give up."

"I'm not giving up. Let's keep going."

A little farther I saw a small animal coming out of its den in the rocks. I silently pointed it out to Lara.

"What is it?" she asked.

"A ground squirrel."

"No, it's not a ground squirrel. I think it's a rock-chuck."

"Whatever it is, we're going to hunt it. Lara, can you whistle?"

A few minutes later we approached the den of the animal with Lara whistling Yankee Doodle. The ground squirrel dived for his hole. Lara kept on walking, still whistling, while I stopped and waited above the den, holding a large boulder. The ground squirrel heard the fading whistling, and thinking all was safe, came out of his den. That's when the bomb fell.

A minute later I proudly lifted it high above my head and yelled, "We got meat! We're going to live!"

I took my knife and cleaned the animal while Lara set out to find fuel for a fire. A few minutes later I heard the rattling of a rattlesnake near where she was standing. She screamed.

"Lara, don't move! Just stand perfectly still. I'm coming over to where you are, but you've got to be still."

Carefully I moved to within a few feet of her, close enough to see a large snake coiled near her feet.

"Don't move, Lara."

"I'm scared," she whispered.

"It's okay to be scared—just don't move."

She started to cry quietly.

"He doesn't want to attack you. As long as you don't press him, he'll leave soon. While we're waiting, let me tell you again about the family of ten I baptized on my mission . . ."

In a few minutes the snake left.

She threw her arms around me and sobbed. I patted her back and kept saying, "It's all right now."

With my arms around her shoulder, we walked back to our fire site.

"I was so scared. I didn't know what to do. Oh, Sam, I love feeling safe in your arms. You were so calm out there."

"Shucks, ma'am, 'tweren't nothing," I joked.

She smiled back through the tears. "All the time you were telling the story about your mission, I kept thinking, 'Sam's right—the snake's going to leave.' Do you know why it left?"

"No, why?"

"It was bored by your story," she laughed through her tears.

A few minutes later I prepared a small nest of tinder, then struck the flint against the blade of the jackknife. After several attempts, a small wisp of smoke curled upward. I picked up the nest and blew life into it. In a few minutes we had a fire going. I took the liver and heart and roasted them over the fire until they were black, then divided them for us.

"Sam, this is the nicest meal I've ever had."

We ate the heart and liver, then put the rest of the animal over the fire.

"I love giving you the food you eat," I said. "It makes me feel strong and useful. In some ways I wish you had to depend on me for all the food you ever ate—that we were an Indian couple long before the white man came. I'd go out to hunt for food. Some days I wouldn't find any, and you'd have to go hungry."

"Wait a minute—what about you? Wouldn't you go hungry too?"

I grinned at her. "No, I need energy for the hunt the next day. Some days I'd kill a deer and bring it in and lay it at your feet. You wouldn't say anything, of course, but there'd be happiness in your eyes. You'd skin the animal and prepare the feast."

124

"Just a minute—what would you be doing while I was skinning the animal?"

"I'd sit with the other braves and tell the story of the hunt."

We both started to laugh and had another sip of water and felt good.

"You're my best friend," I said contentedly.

"You're mine too, Sam. You make me feel safe and protected, and I love that feeling. Look at your arms," she said, running her fingers up my arm. "They're so strong. And your shoulders—I love your shoulders. Sometimes more than anything I just want to be safe in a man's arms, the way I feel now with you."

"We're a team, you know that?" I said. "A man and a woman are equal, but they're not the same. But if we combine our talents, we can do anything."

I took some grease from the prairie dog and rubbed it on Lara's sunburned nose.

"Sometimes," I confessed, "I hear voices in my head. One of the voices is from grade school. It says, 'You gonna let a girl beat you?' You know what I'm going to start telling that voice? I'll say, 'It's okay to let this girl do better than me—because we're a team, and a team may scrimmage, but it doesn't count as a game. It just makes us better.'"

"Oh, Sam, I adore you. You're everything I've ever wanted to find in a man."

I gave some of the hindquarters of the roasted meat to Lara.

"We got through this," I said proudly. "We can get through anything. I've got Self-Knowledge now. You know, I'm not always going to be just a computer programmer. I've been thinking about starting my own company to sell small computers to homes. It'll help them budget their money, remind them when their car needs servicing, and turn down the thermostat at night. It'll be fantastic."

"You can do it, Sam."

"Oh sure, I know it'll be hard at first," I said, munching away on the meat on the other part of the hindquarters. "Lara, it's a dog-eat-dog world out there."

"But you'll succeed, I know you will."

"Yes, because I have Self-Knowledge. You know what, the better I feel about myself, the more I love you. Lara, I want you by my side all the way."

She looked down the trail.

"It's not wide enough."

"No—life's way. Will you marry me?"

She sighed. "Oh, wow, will I!"

"That's what I asked."

"I will, I will!"

We kissed. Our lips stuck together.

"May I have some water now?" she asked.

"No—but I'll give you my special pebble."

"Sam, please, just a little water. Kissing you out here is like sucking on popcorn."

"Oh, all right."

After four gulps, I had to pull the canteen away from her again.

Then we tried another kiss.

The shadows crept across the canyon floor and we knew the jeep would soon be coming, so we started down to the mouth of our canyon.

"Brock says they're going to have a special hike next summer—fifty miles without food or water in the California desert. It sounds wonderful, doesn't it? Maybe we can save up for it."

Lara was wrong. The trail was wide enough for her to walk by my side as we strolled hand in hand down the trail. "Did you happen to read *Time* magazine last week?" she asked as we walked.

"No, I missed it."

"Want me to tell you what was in it?" she asked.

"Sure."

"On page one there was an ad for Ford Granada. And on page two . . ."

126

Chapter Thirteen

We drove home the next day and announced our engagement. Our parents were delighted.

When Steve found out, he invited us to dinner. He was alone; he said his wife was visiting her parents.

I had him tell how he began with no money and how things grew. Then I explained my dream of having my own store that sold small computers.

"Just do it—take the plunge."

During the dessert he made his play. "Lara's told me she'll probably quit when you two get married. Why don't you let her work for a while? It'll give you time to start your own business. You'd be on the way to your goals, and I'd keep the best salesperson I've ever seen."

"Well, I don't know. I've got a boy who needs a mother."

"I'm giving you the chance of a lifetime. You're not going to just sit on your goals, are you? C'mon, Sam, be an eagle."

A few days later we decided to follow Steve's advice. I would work at the computer center until the middle of January, then Lara and I would get married. I'd have my grand opening in February. Lara would continue to work until the store began paying enough for us to get by.

And so reluctantly I became an eagle.

We were married in January in the Salt Lake Temple. Many of the single adults were in the sealing room with us.

From seven to eight-thirty that night we had a reception at the church.

But there was a second reception, from nine to ten, that was more fun. Lara and I wore our clown costumes for a reception just for the single adults.

We went through the courtship of Wilbur the Clown and Fran the Frazzled Fraulein. I knelt in front of her in the classical proposal stance.

"I want your hand."

"Vas ist das?" she asked.

"I want your hand," I pleaded, grabbing at the plastic hand sticking out of her sleeve and pulling it out.

She screamed and I ran away. She started to recite a poem in German. I picked up a large push broom and crept up on her. The second the broom touched her feet, she fell forward.

Sister Hilton, the announcer for our shows, asked me why I'd done that.

"I wanted to sweep her off her feet!" I yelled.

The part we enjoyed the best was the sharing of the cake. I opened my mouth and she shoved an enormous piece into it. Without a word I did the same to her. What was left over, I smeared on her nose.

She pointed at something inside the cake. When I bent over to look, she pushed my head into it.

After wiping off the mess, we got serious. We told them how we felt about our experiences with the single adults. It was getting pretty mushy so Sister Hilton had us open our presents. The first one was a whoopy pillow, one that makes strange noises when someone sits on it. Every gift was a gag.

128

Last of all we sang "Till We Meet Again," had a prayer, and left.

When I started the car, a siren wailed crazily until I could open the hood, find the gimmick, and pull it loose. Then came a nervous drive up the canyon to my uncle's cabin in the woods where we were to spend our first night together.

*   *   *   *   *   *

I sat on the bed in my pajamas and listened to the sound of Lara's shower. Looking at the fireplace, I thought how romantic it would be to have a nice fire going when she came out.

Still in pajamas, I put on a pair of my uncle's boots and went outside to the woodpile, cut some kindling, and carried it inside. I found a pile of old newspapers and magazines, crumpled and threw some into the fireplace, then carefully laid the wood on top and set the paper on fire.

Then I remembered the axe was still outside and went to get it. As long as I was there, I decided, I'd chop some more wood for later. Five minutes later when I went inside, the entire room was filled with smoke. I'd forgotten to open the draft.

Grabbing the wood that was still smoking, I ran it outside and tossed it in a snowbank. In the process I slid on some ice and fell, twisting my ankle. Limping back, I wiped my forehead, spreading black over my face. Then I opened all the windows to get the smoke out.

That's when Lara opened the bathroom door expecting to find her Prince Charming regally attired in lounging robe, about to offer her a glass of ginger ale. Instead she saw a guy wearing sooty pajamas, hiking boots, his face blackened like a coal miner, and the room filled with thick smoke. I was bent over, looking up the chimney, still searching for the draft to the fireplace.

"Good grief!" she gasped.

I limped toward her, no doubt resembling Captain Ahab.

"Hi there."

"Is this a family wedding ritual?" she asked.

"A few technical difficulties."

She ran back to the bathroom, closed the door, and locked it.

"Don't worry!" I yelled. "I'll have things fixed in no time. Do you want to help me?"

"Are you kidding?" she answered through the door. "Wearing a negligee? If I knew this is what we were going to do, I'd have worn thermal underwear and a backpack."

"Wait in there until I call you. Okay?"

"Okay," she said faintly, sounding as if she were about to cry.

"Do you want to read a magazine while you're waiting?"

"I guess so."

"It's the special issue they do every year about pheasants."

I slid the magazine under the door and went back to work. I found a summer fan and turned it on near the open door to try and clear out the smoke. Eventually I found the draft, opened it, and repeated the process of starting a fire again. Within a few minutes there was a small fire going, but the temperature was still below freezing. It would have to do. I couldn't wait all night.

Back to the bathroom door. "Lara, the fire is going now. You can come out."

"Can I just finish this one article?" she asked.

I sighed. "I guess so—if that's what you really want to do."

I went back to the fireplace and threw another log on.

She opened the door and realized how cold it was in

130

the room. There was a blur of white as she raced across the room and into bed.

"Ooooh!"

"What's wrong?"

"I'm not going to tell you what a shock these cold sheets are." She pulled the covers up to her chin. Then she looked at me and started to laugh.

"You look like a chimney sweep," she grinned.

"Do you know it's good luck to kiss a chimney sweep?"

"No way. You go wash your face and hands."

"Yes, mother," I said, heading for the bathroom.

"Oh Sam, toss me out that magazine, will you? I never knew pheasants were so interesting."

When I returned, the room was just slightly warmer. I walked to the bed and sat down. "Lara, we should have our first family prayer now."

"A kneeling prayer?" she asked, reluctant to leave the warm bed.

"Maybe not. How about a prayer with us just sitting here?"

After the prayer, she looked at me and smiled nervously.

"Sam, could we talk a little?"

"About what?"

"I don't know—something—anything. I know—ask me anything about ring-necked pheasants." She had the blankets pulled up to her chin with both hands.

I smiled. She nervously smiled back.

"I'll be right back," I said suddenly.

"Where are you going, Sam?"

"Out to the car. I've got a tape of 'Mystery Theater' we can listen to."

*   *   *   *   *   *

Sometime during the night, I woke up and put another log on the fire and then went to back to bed. Seeing a couple of glasses of water on the nightstand, I figured Lara had set them out after I'd fallen asleep so we wouldn't have to get out of bed and get our feet cold. I took one glass and drank it. Since there wasn't much water in it, I drank hers too.

What a wife, I thought. She thinks of everything.

The next morning we lay in bed and talked while we waited for the room to warm up. Finally she turned to the water glasses. "Where are my contact lenses?"

"What?"

"I forgot my soaking case. I put one in each glass last night after you'd fallen asleep. What did you do with them?"

I shut my eyes and shook my head.

"Sam, where are they? I can't see a thing without them."

"I'm sorry to tell you this but—" I started to laugh uncontrollably.

"What happened? I don't have another pair."

"Lara, your contact lenses have . . . passed away."

*   *   *   *   *   *

We left that morning for Idaho and a reception planned for that night.

"Hello," Lara said warmly to the blur standing in front of her in the receiving line.

"Lara, why are you squinting so?" an elderly aunt asked her. "Please introduce me to your husband."

"This is my husband."

"Well, tell him who I am!"

Lara leaned over to stare at the face.

"Oh! This is my Aunt Lynne."

Later that night, just after the reception was over, I heard two older men talking about us.

"They say he ate her contact lenses. Why would he do that?"

132

"Who knows about kids these days—always after some new thrill. It's TV that's done it—wrecked the whole generation."

Chapter Fourteen

Don't start a new business the same time you begin a marriage.

The next few months were characterized by my losing a little money each week, and Lara becoming a little more successful at her store. Before long her closet contained several dresses she'd won in the monthly contests.

By April she was paying for our food and rent and utilities. I was dumping all my money into my business and watching it slowly sink.

Our marriage floundered too. Some couples, when they have problems, argue. Lara and I became polite.

Once when I was a young adult, someone told me that one of the presidents of the Church and his wife had never argued. In my post-mission enthusiasm, I'd vowed my wife and I would also never argue. In time this was altered to mean I would avoid even talking about problems in my marriage.

We quit talking about anything important. Instead we dwelt on the trivial.

"Sam, I'm going to take some of my things to the cleaners. If you have anything, I'll take it for you."

I looked up from my newspaper. "No thanks."

"Don't you have anything that needs cleaning?"

"I don't know. If I do, I can drop it by tomorrow."

"I'll be happy to drop it by now."

"What cleaners are you going to?"

"Mr. Nifty. It's the closest."

"I prefer taking mine to Busy Bee."

"Okay, I'll take both of ours to Busy Bee."

"That's all right—you needn't bother."

"It's no bother."

No answer from me. I appeared to be interested in what I was reading.

"Why don't you want me to take your clothes to the cleaners?" she asked.

"It's out of your way. I know you're very busy at work these days."

She sighed. "I'm not at work now. I'm home, about to take some clothes to the cleaners. Just show me which of yours to take."

I finally looked up from my paper. "I think it's better if you take yours to Mr. Nifty, and I take mine to Busy Bee."

She stared at me as I burrowed deeper into my newspaper.

Finally she shrugged her shoulders. "Okay, Sam. 'Bye."

Late one night as I slipped into bed after watching the late-night movie on TV, I could tell she was silently crying in the dark. I lay there and listened to her, hoping she'd quit so I could to go to sleep, but she didn't. Finally I got up, went back to the living room, turned on the TV, and an hour later fell asleep on the couch.

But we didn't argue. Isn't it wonderful we didn't argue?

The sad thing was that we never really defined the problem. Later she told me she thought I was unhappy I'd ever married her because she wasn't like Charly. That wasn't it. The problem was that I couldn't take her success.

In time we learned to avoid talking about work. I sheltered her from my failures, and she kindly sheltered me from her success.

In May I decided that if the customers wouldn't come to see me, then I'd go to the customers.

"Yeah, whadaya want?" the giant at the door growled.

"I'm with Samtrex Home Computer Service."

"So what?"

"You may have seen our ad in Saturday's paper. I'd like to tell you about our new line of small computers."

He swore, then asked, "What do I need a computer for?"

"You can use it to budget your money."

"Budget money? Come in."

The giant had a wife.

"You talk to her about budgeting!" he roared, pointing a hairy arm at his wife, a tired woman in a housecoat.

Moving aside some clothes from the couch, I sat down, smiled hopefully, and began. "In this time of rapid inflation, I'm sure you know how difficult it is to effectively monitor where the money goes. The Sussex 4S-KB computer can give you instant feedback on the status of your various accounts. Let me show you how the budget program works. First you set up various accounts—a house payment account, a food account, clothing, utilities—"

"Snowmobile!" she yelled, glaring at her husband.

I stopped.

"He has to go out and buy a snowmobile! Doesn't even talk to me about it. What a stupid thing to do!"

"Not if it gets me away from you during the winters!" he yelled.

" . . . a snowmobile account," I added. "With the Sussex 4S-KB home computer, you'll gain control of your money—"

"Drapes!" he shouted at her.

"We need drapes," she argued.

"We don't need drapes! We got drapes!"

"You want gray drapes? You want torn drapes? You want people to see our torn gray drapes?"

"What people? Your mother, you mean? She's not people!"

" . . . the Sussex 4S-KB computer can also perform other essential services in the home."

"Guns!" she shrieked. "How many guns you gonna buy? What do you need so many guns for? There are army posts with less guns than you got!"

I excused myself and left. They didn't even notice.

"A six-hundred-dollar vacuum cleaner!" he shouted at her as I escaped.

*   *   *   *   *   *

A day later, in another section of town, the door was opened by someone I hadn't seen since junior high school. Then he was Punky Johnson. Punky sat next to me in math class in eighth grade. A good day for Punky was when he figured out what page the teacher was on.

He recognized me and invited me in. It was a large two-story house, elegant and tasteful.

"I don't suppose you go by Punky anymore, do you?"

He laughed. "Not anymore. They call me Jim now. I run Johnson Construction. Ever hear of it?"

"Sure—you guys are working on every big project in town."

He smiled. "We're doing okay. Oh, this is my wife, Shelley. She was Miss Utah a few years ago."

I stood to greet the stunning Mrs. Punky.

"Shelley, if it weren't for Sam, I'd still be in junior high. He was the smartest one in math. Sam, what are you doing now?"

I cleared my throat, trying to decide whether to exaggerate or to outright lie.

"Well, I've got my own company now—Samtrex Computers. We sell small computers for the home—and for business too."

"Hey, isn't that great? I always knew you'd succeed. I'll bet you're really raking in the money, hey?"

No, I thought. Why do you think I'm going door-to-door?

"Picking up all the time." I matched his grin.

"You know, I'd buy a bunch from you, I really would, but another guy beat you to it, from a company called IBM."

A few minutes later, after being told what his gross was last year, I left.

Life's not fair. If a guy can make it who can't even find the circumference of a circle, where's the justice?

*   *   *   *   *   *

One day after work I visited Jon and Shirley. She was pregnant and looked more beautiful than I'd ever seen her before. She made the mistake of asking me how my business was going.

"It's a disaster."

"How are you and Lara getting by, then?" she asked.

"She's making money like crazy," I said. "She's assistant manager now, you know."

"No wife of mine is ever going to work," Jon said emphatically.

"It's only temporary."

"I'm not surprised you're losing money," Jon said. "This is probably the worst time in history to start a business. Inflation, recession. It's the politicians that've done it. The way things are today, it wouldn't surprise me if you went bankrupt."

Shirley sent him a warning glance.

"Jon, it just takes a little time to get a business going," she said, trying to soften Jon's impact.

"But what'll he do if his business fails before then?" he asked.

I shrugged my shoulders. "I don't know. It's not just the money. I'm losing my self-confidence."

"I knew a guy like that once," Jon said. "Couldn't do anything right."

"Jon!" Shirley complained.

"I was just telling about a guy I knew once."

"He doesn't need to know. He came here for some encouragement from us."

"It's not my fault he starts a business in times like this, is it?"

A few minutes later, Jon took out his checkbook. "I want to buy something from you for thirty dollars. That's all we've got left this month."

"You don't need to do that," I said.

"What can I buy for thirty dollars?"

"Not much, I'm afraid. We have an instruction manual for one of our computers that costs about that much."

"Good, I'll take it."

"But it won't do any good without the computer."

"I'll put it in my bookcase—the one I built."

He handed me the check. "Now let me show you the crib I made for my son when he's born."

*   *   *   *   *   *

A few days later, with no business all day, I closed up early and went home. Lara was still at work and Adam was with my parents. I walked into the silent apartment, looked at the stack of bills Lara would end up paying, then went into our bedroom and knelt down, feeling very depressed.

The pattern of my life is to do everything on my own until things are so fouled up that I'm in a hopeless trap; then I ask God for help.

"Remember me? I'm the guy who only comes to you when things are impossible. Well, it's that time again."

I'd prayed about it before—little thirty-second vignettes in a routine list of requests to "bless my business to do well."

This prayer was different because I first told Him

what the problem was, then told Him what I was willing to do, and then asked for what I needed Him to do. The difference was what I committed to do.

It was a long prayer, and even though I don't know if He has an interest in small computers, I took Him in as a partner.

When Lara showed up with Adam, I didn't tell her anything. My outside reason was I didn't want her to worry.

She brought home a dress she'd won. It was very nice and I hated it.

*   *   *   *   *   *

In church we were model newlyweds. Bright, cheerful in a crowd, we both tried desperately to find safe, trivial topics when we were alone.

We attended a Sunday School class in family relations. One day the bishop came to talk to the class.

"Most of the problems in a marriage revolve around poor communication. Much of the time I find the wife wants to come in for counseling, but her husband won't admit there's even a problem."

On the way home, Lara asked, "What would you think about our going to the bishop?"

"What for?" I asked.

"Our problems."

"What problems?" I snickered. "We don't have any problems. We don't even argue."

"We never talk anymore."

"We're talking now."

"Sam, just tell me what's wrong. Is it something I'm doing wrong?"

"There's nothing wrong."

"You're saving stamps, aren't you," she said.

"I don't know what you mean."

140

"You're holding in all your frustrations, like saving trading stamps, and someday you're going to redeem them all at once. I read about it once."

I scoffed. "You read too much—there's nothing wrong. Everything's fine."

The best way to describe our life was perfunctory. Everything we did was perfunctory.

*　　　*　　　*　　　*　　　*　　　*

It was on a Friday night in May when the stamp redemption center opened for business.

"How'd it go today?" she asked after supper.

"Fine," I said bleakly.

"Sam, what's wrong?"

"Nothing's wrong," I said, feeling heroic.

I lay down and played with Adam while Lara read a book.

Adam went outside to play on his swings.

She set down her book and turned to me. "There's something I need to talk to you about. Today Steve asked me to manage one of his new stores. It would mean a fantastic raise."

"And you told him no, right?"

"I told him I'd talk to you about it."

"All right, tomorrow you can tell him no."

"Can we at least talk about it?"

"What's there to talk about?"

"We need the money now, don't we? At least until your business gets going."

"The answer is no."

"I'll arrange things so it won't take any more time."

"One store manager in this family is enough," I grumbled.

"Are you against it because I'd be earning more than you?"

I exploded. "A ten-year-old kid with a lemonade stand is earning more than me!"

She looked at me in shock. "I thought things were going okay."

"Do you want to know the sum total of today's business? A lady came in looking for directions, a man came by asking for a donation, and two kids came in asking if I had R2-D2 in the store!"

"Sam, why haven't you told me this before?"

"I didn't want you to worry."

"Why not? Is it the man's place to worry? I'm a part of this marriage too. Why won't you let me into your life? You walk around being so noble all the time, but it leaves me on the outside of your life. You're supposed to talk to me. I love you. The only reason I'm working is for you."

"Oh c'mon, Lara, you can tell your church friends that, but I know better. You get your kicks out of competition. Face it, you're hooked on success."

She let out a long sigh and nervously ruffled her hair, then very calmly continued. "Let's see if I understand —you don't want me to be a manager, right?"

"How would you feel if you were me? Asking you for lunch money every morning."

"That's not true, and you know it. All the money goes into one checking account. It's your money too."

"Why can't you stay home and be a housewife? Why do I always have to be running to catch up with you?"

She looked at me as if I were a total stranger. "Good grief, is that the way you feel? Maybe you're right, maybe it's better when we don't talk. I feel so much anger coming from you."

"I'm not angry," I said angrily.

"Yes you are—your body language reveals the way you really feel."

"Body language? That's from a book, isn't it? Always trying to improve your mind—you can't let well enough alone, can you."

She closed her eyes and rested her head in both hands. A minute later, she looked up at me again. "What

142

else is bothering you? C'mon, let it all spill out."

"Okay, I will!" I snapped. "I'm tired of my son being dumped off every day with his grandmother! I want us to be a normal family where I earn the money and you spend it. And just once, is it asking too much for you to make gingerbread cookies for my son? Is that asking too much? With sugar, Lara, with sugar! Are you listening to me?"

She looked at me, then quietly replied, "Everyone in the block's listening to you."

"Why won't you do what I say? Whatever happened to 'follow the priesthood'?"

"Sam, you tell me first what happened to 'gentleness, meekness, and love unfeigned.' "

"That does it!" I roared. "Not only don't I want you to be a store manager, now I don't even want you to work anymore!"

"You mean quit my job?"

"That's it—quit your job and be a wife and mother."

She pursed her lips and said evenly, "It doesn't make any sense for me to quit right now."

"I've made up my mind."

"We'll talk later."

"We'll talk now!"

She sighed. "All right—you feel threatened by my working, right?"

"Don't try any of that listening jazz on me either!"

I rushed to the closet and got Adam's sweatshirt.

"Where are you going?"

"I'm going out with my son! You remember him, don't you? He's that little person we drop off every morning on our way to work!"

"Please tell me where you're going."

"To a movie—is that all right?" I barked.

I stormed outside, lifted Adam from his swing, and set him in the front seat of the car, started to get in, stopped, checked my wallet, muttered to myself, and marched back inside.

"What's wrong?" she asked.

Sheepishly I looked at her and admitted, "I need money for the movie."

She handed me her pocketbook. "Take all you want."

I took a ten dollar bill, smiled slightly, and asked, "Is it okay if we get popcorn too?"

She smiled back, just a little.

"Lara, I love you," I said.

"Do you, Sam?"

"I think so."

I hurried to the car. I think I left her crying.

Half an hour into the movie Adam fell asleep. I numbly watched it twice. By the time we got out, it was eleven-thirty.

Either Lara was asleep or else she was faking it. I put Adam in a nighttime diaper, put him in his crib, then quietly slipped into bed. All night long I was careful not even to touch Lara's feet. We both clung to the safety of the opposite edges of the mattress.

The next morning I got up early, decided to skip work, woke Adam, dressed him, and we left.

We drove to my parents' house. Dad was up, reading scriptures. I walked in, said hello, and told him I needed something in the garage. Then I went and retrieved my last model plane from the rafters.

We stopped for a box of donuts for breakfast, then went to the park. I parked near the Ferris wheel.

While Adam explored the area, I sat down on a bench and took the picture of Charly from my wallet and looked at her again, letting the memories flood my mind. A few weeks earlier I'd started taking it out in the store when I was alone, which was most of the time. The rockier my relationship with Lara, the more I thought about Charly.

Then I went to the car and got the plane. We sat on the lawn and waited for someone to help us launch it.

"Plane go high in the sky?" he said, except it came out "pane."

"We need somebody to help us."

144

"Mommy Lara help," he said, except it became "Ra-ra."

"She's working today. Saturday is her big day at the store."

"She help."

"Maybe, but I can't ask her." I shook my head in frustration. "Adam, let me give you a little advice. You're going to be a man someday. A man must never waver, a man must set his course in life . . . "

"Mommy Rara help fy pane in the sky," he said strongly.

"A man must be strong, and his wife must be . . . "

I stopped.

"His wife must be . . . " I shook my head. I didn't know anymore.

"Pane go high?" Adam asked.

"Very high—the pain is very high right now."

He found a bug to torment. I sat and thought.

A few minutes later I tried thinking out loud. "My great-grandfather—now there was a man for you. He was a pioneer with three wives when he crossed the plains. There he was, out in the wilderness, women to the right of him, women to the left of him, but he kept going. Across the wilderness they went, him at the head of his wagon, fighting the wind and the rain and the burning sun, listening to all his wives' suggestions. What a man he was, Adam. That was a time to be alive, when men were men, and women stayed in the covered wagon. Now women are everywhere . . . "

"Where Mommy Rara?"

"Winning herself another dress. Adam, tell me something. Do you miss not having gingerbread cookies?"

"Cookie?" he asked, his eyes getting big.

"Not just any cookie—a gingerbread man with little frosting buttons and eyes and smile. I'm talking about your real, homemade gingerbread cookie. You're growing up without them. Do you miss that?"

"Adam want cookie."

"Have a donut, okay? I had gingerbread cookies when I was a boy. Your grandmother made them for me. She didn't work at a store, you know. She stayed home. When I'd come home from play, she'd give me gingerbread cookies. Adam, let me tell you, they were fun to eat. Sometimes I'd bite its little gingerbread head off in one bite."

"I want fy pane in the sky."

"We will, we will. In a few minutes somebody'll come along and help."

I held him in my lap and talked. "I don't really know what to tell you now about being a man. Things change. A woman could be president of the United States. Think of that, Adam. Maybe a woman like Lara. She's so smart. That's my problem. I'm afraid she's better than me in every way, that she'll always have the best ideas and suggestions. What would happen to our family if I always did what she suggested? Even if she was right? Don't you see what a position I'd be placing myself in? Everyone'd think I was weak. Of course, if we always made the right decision, I guess that'd be good. Maybe it wouldn't be so bad—except I'm supposed to be the boss. How am I the boss if I always do what she suggests?"

"I want Mommy Rara fy pane."

"Once I thought I had Self-Knowledge. Now I can't even remember what it was. Sometimes, Adam, I'm scared. You might as well know that now. Men aren't always strong—there was only one John Wayne."

He left to explore on his own.

Ten minutes later I looked over to see him tipping up a beer can to drink any leftovers. I hurried to stop him.

On our way to the garbage can I continued our discussion. "I think I've forgotten something, and that's to tell you to follow the Savior. He's the best example of manhood in the world. And follow the prophets and apostles, and . . . watch your father."

That's when it hit me.

"Adam, we've got to go home and find Mommy Lara and apologize."

146

I threw the plane in the trunk and we left the park. Two blocks from home, we saw her riding toward us on an old dirt bike belonging to a neighbor boy.

"Mommy Rara funny," Adam chuckled.

I stopped the car, partially blocking a lane of traffic, and ran to her across the street on the sidewalk. She was wearing jeans, a Western sport shirt, and sneakers. I loved her just that way, without anything from the store.

"I'm sorry! I'm really sorry! Can you forgive me?"

She dropped the bike and threw her arms around me and cried.

A cab driver, having to maneuver around my car, leaned out and yelled at me.

I nodded my head, but didn't move.

Lara continued to cry.

Adam starting honking the horn.

We broke apart and walked across the street. I threw the bike on top of the car and we returned it to our neighbor.

Lara was still in the car when I came back. I looked at my watch. "You'd better get ready for work."

"I'm not going to work today," she said.

"Me either. Can you come and play with us?"

She gave me a cautious grin. "I'll have to ask my mother first."

A few minutes later, back at the park, I showed her how to start the engine and launch the plane. Then I went to the controls and we had lift-off.

Our plane was up and flying. I motioned for her to come to me and I showed her how to fly it. I stood in back of her with my arms around her, both of us holding the controls, feeling her warmth and catching the slight accent of her perfume.

We kept it in simple patterns until it ran out of gas.

By this time, Adam had reopened the donut box and sampled each one. His face was covered with jelly.

"That's his breakfast?" she gently asked.

"I got him fruit-filled so he'd get his vitamin C."

We smiled politely at each other.

147

"Lara, I'm sorry."

"You made me feel so bad last night."

"I know."

"No, you don't know. But sit down—I'm going to tell you."

I sat down on the grass with her.

"I tried," she said, "I really tried to be everything people expected me to be—a model housewife, a good cook, an efficient worker at the store, a new mother for Adam, a source of income for you so your business could get a start, a dependable person in my callings in church. I tried to do it all, and I almost made it, didn't I? Almost—I had everyone pleased, everyone but you, everyone but me. Sam, I can't be Wonder Woman anymore."

"I've never heard you sound like this before."

"Like what?"

"Vulnerable," I finally said.

"But that's what I am."

"Me too. Ask my creditors, they'll tell you."

"I want our marriage to work out," she said seriously.

"Are we talking about that?"

"I think we are."

"Why are we?"

"Because I'm scared. After you left last night, Steve called. He asked what we'd decided about my becoming a manager. I started to cry and told him about our argument and about your leaving. I must've sounded pretty upset, because he said he was coming over. A few minutes later I was in the bathroom looking in the mirror, wondering what to do for my eyes so I'd look decent for him. Suddenly I saw how things might go. He'd come over and I'd tell him my complaints, and he'd sympathize and tell me how much he admires me, and how sorry he is that things aren't working out. Then he'd go home. Someday at work maybe he'd ask me out for lunch so we could talk. He'd tell me about his ex-wife, how she never really understood him. And it'd go on and on until gradually I'd feel closer to him than I do to you. Sam, I know where that can end."

I nodded my head.

"All this time I was staring at myself in the mirror, seeing weaknesses in me I never dreamed were there. Sam, I enjoy his compliments. He's given me ten times as many as you have. By the time I heard the doorbell, I was scared to death—not of him—I was scared of me. I couldn't face him. He kept ringing the bell. Finally I opened the door a crack and told him I couldn't see him, that I just wanted him to leave. And so he left."

I let out a secret sigh of relief.

"This morning," she continued, "your dad called and said you'd left Adam's sweatshirt at the house on your way to the park. I went next door and borrowed a bike and set out to find you. That's when you came along. So here I am," she said with a hint of a smile. "I've just avoided a path that for me might have eventually led to adultery. And what have you been doing lately?"

"Me? I'm into bankruptcy these days."

"What a pair we are," she sniffled one last time.

"I love your face," I said.

"Is that important to this discussion?"

"No, but I just thought you'd like to know."

"I do—thanks. Anyway, I called the store today and told them I wasn't coming in, so I'm yours for the day. What shall we do?"

"Tonight let's listen to 'Mystery Theater'."

She nodded her head and grinned.

"We don't have to if you don't want to," I added quickly.

She started to giggle. "I do love a good mystery now and then."

"Me too," I beamed.

"There's one other thing," she said. "I've decided to do what you counsel me."

"No you won't."

"Try me," she challenged.

"Stand on your head."

"Don't be silly."

"I knew it."

"I mean about my job. I'll quit work, stay home, try to get pregnant, and make gingerbread cookies—every day, if you want."

"Of course you could quit working," I said, slightly off-balance, wondering if she meant she'd try to get pregnant every day as well as bake the cookies. "Realistically speaking, though, this isn't a good time for the extra income to stop."

"Realistically speaking," she countered, "the income from my job isn't extra. We need it all. And I'm afraid we always will and I'll never be able to quit."

"But you enjoy your work, and you're good at it."

"Good? I'm fantastic! And it's fun to be the modern woman, liberated in the business world. But it isn't liberation if I can't ever break loose. I don't want to work anymore."

"Are you saying that just because you're afraid of what might happen between you and Steve? I have more confidence in you than that. The problem wasn't that you were working. It was that we'd quit communicating. And that was my fault."

"That's not the only reason," she said reflectively. "Last night I decided I don't want to run competition with you. When you leave for work in the morning, I want you to know you have a little bit of heaven waiting for you when you come home."

"Why should you be the one to do all the changing?" I asked. "I can learn to adjust to your working."

"I want to quit my job."

"You're just surrendering?"

"It's not a war, Sam. Why can't I have the freedom to change my priorities? I want to spend more time with Adam and I want some children of my own. Maybe after our children are grown, I'll go back to work."

"Grown? They haven't even been conceived yet."

She smiled coyly. "I'm sure we can work that out."

"But if you quit," I said, suddenly worried, "what'll we do for food and rent?"

"My man'll provide for our needs," she said, full of confidence.

"Me?" I croaked.

"Hey, where's all that Self-Knowledge? I saw you in the desert, killing our supper with only a song and a rock, starting a fire with no matches, saving me from a rattlesnake. You can do anything you want."

"You believe that?"

"Sure, you're terrific. Cute, too."

"But you'd just quit your job?" I asked weakly.

"Sam, why are we arguing? Yesterday you asked me to quit working. Today I say I will. Now you're trying to talk me out of it."

I shrugged my shoulders and grinned. "It's the curse of some marriages. It happens whenever the husband and wife are equally compromising. To escape, one of us has to be reasonable and the other stubborn. Which do you choose?"

"I'll take reasonable."

"Rats, I wanted that."

She started to laugh. "Oh well, you can be reasonable if you want."

"No no—not if you want it that badly."

Adam dragged the box of partially eaten donuts over to us. We tasted the fragments, or at least I did.

"Are we ever going to figure this out?" I asked. "Let's start with the basics. You're a woman and I'm a man."

"Nice combination, don't you think?"

"And you're my wife."

"Considering the past few months, I'd better be."

"And I'm your husband."

"So far it all ties together quite logically, doesn't it?"

"In olden times, I'd rule and reign over you. But those days are gone forever. So what do I do?"

"You preside, Sam. You're the president of our family, and I'm your vice-president."

"How do you know that?"

"I read your priesthood manual last night."

"You did? Is that all right to do?"

"Why not? You preside—so preside for me, Sam."

"Vice-president, what do we do about your working?"

"Mr. President, what would be wrong with following the counsel of our Church leaders?"

I sighed. "I've started a journal—isn't that enough?"

"They tell us no success can compensate for failure in the home. They say the most important of the Lord's work we'll ever do will be within the walls of our own home. So why don't I stay home with Adam and make gingerbread cookies and have some children?"

"You'd make gingerbread cookies?" I wavered.

"Dozens and dozens."

"Oh, I don't know, Lara," I moaned. "You've got what it takes to be a big success in business. I don't want to deny you any opportunities. Are you sure you want to quit?"

"I'm sure."

"Promise me one thing. If you do quit, promise me you'll never worry about which brand of paper towels absorbs more spills."

"I promise. Is it a deal then?"

"Let me think about it."

We couldn't take looking at Adam's messy face any longer, so we found a drinking fountain and cleaned him up, then took a little walk.

"Lara, I don't need gingerbread cookies anymore. What I need is help with my business. The computer business is one of the fastest growing industries in America, but I'm losing my shirt. You're the genius at marketing. I need your help."

She sighed. "You'll never know how good that sounds to me."

"Well, it's true. Without you, what am I?"

"Let's not find out," she said. Then we enjoyed a long kiss.

"Gonna fly the plane again, huh?"

We broke apart to face the boy who used to help me launch my planes.

"Yes, we are," I blushed.

He had his little calculator with him again.

"You still stay up late building model planes?" he asked.

"Not anymore. Now," I stammered, "now I sleep at night."

"And listen to the radio," Lara teased. "What's that?"

"Electronic football."

We looked at it. It buzzed and whistled.

"You gonna crash this plane too?" he asked.

"No, not this one."

"I'll be going then. See you around."

We walked to the swings and gave Adam a ride. I had Lara stand in front of him and try to catch his toes.

We were a family now.

She asked me to pretend she was a customer and to try to sell her a computer. After ten minutes I quit and asked her impressions.

"The truth?" she asked.

"I guess so."

"The part that wasn't boring was intimidating."

"It was?"

"Computers intimidate people."

"That's strange—I should've known. I understand intimidation."

"And another thing. Did I actually hear you say 'floppy-disk drive'?"

"It's just a term computer people use."

"Well, don't use it around your customers. Sam, you have to make it fun. You talk about a computer for budgeting. That's really boring. Can't you sell something involving a computer that's easy and fun? What about that boy with his electronic football? There must be some kind of computer in there, but he doesn't care. He's having fun."

"Sure, there are computer games available. Once a

person has a computer, he can order the games. But first he has to buy a computer."

"Why? How about leasing or renting them? And how about starting a computer game-of-the-month club? And why are you just concentrating on computers in the home? Why aren't you marketing more to small businesses?"

"I don't know, I don't know!" I laughed. "But I love your questions. Look, Lara, why don't you quit your job and be my marketing consultant?"

"That's what I've been trying to tell you—I *am* your consultant! It goes with the wedding license."

"No extra cost?"

"None whatsoever."

"What a bargain you are!" I shouted.

"I know it!" she laughed. "I'm fantastic, aren't I! And I'm all yours!"

We held hands. Adam figured it was a signal to play ring-around-a-rosy, and so we did, the three of us giggling as we fell down.

"Again," Adam insisted, trying to pull us up again.

We played until he got bored and wandered back to the swing.

"So what about your job if you're my consultant?" I asked.

"Sam, let me quit. Adam and I will think about computers while we're making gingerbread cookies."

"Instead of being a consultant, I'm prepared to make you a full partner in the business. I'm sure my other partner would approve. In fact, this is probably what he's been waiting for."

"Who's your other partner?" she asked.

"God."

We strolled over to Adam. It felt good to have my arm around her waist.

"I won't be able to pay you anything for a while," I said, "but there are some interesting fringe benefits to the job," I said, bringing her in close to me.

"I'll take the job," she smiled.

Later that day we went to the library. She picked up a book dealing with model planes and another about computers. I checked out one that taught how to listen and communicate.

Two days later for family home evening, with Lara quoting sections she'd memorized, we both learned to do the loop-the-loop without crashing.

*   *   *   *   *   *

This is how the week went after Lara quit her job.

Monday. When I walked into our apartment after work, there was the delicious smell of gingerbread cookies. Adam sat at the kitchen table, flour on his nose, eating the arms off a gingerbread man. I kissed Lara and she gave me a cookie.

After supper, we played ring-around-a-rosy and Lara told a flannelboard story for family home evening.

Tuesday. At home after work, I conferred with my business partner. During the day she had phoned several stores in California and talked to their managers. She had also had an afternoon meeting with a banker to see how feasible it would be to lease computers with part of the customer's payment going toward purchase. And she had written down some ideas for a nationwide computer game-of-the-month club.

Wednesday. I met my public relations and marketing agent. She had set up some presentations for me to give to some local service clubs.

Thursday. This was her day and she'd spent it riding horses with a friend. She walked bow-legged all night.

Friday. When I walked in the apartment, she met me with incense and wearing a Japanese kimono. Adam was conveniently having supper with his grandparents. She gave me a pair of Oriental-style pajamas to put on.

"What for?" I asked, still off-balance.

"I think it's important for us to learn about other cultures, don't you?" she said, giving me a sly grin.

Two hours later we had supper on the floor around our coffee table. I had trouble with my chopsticks and kept dropping rice.

"Happy?" she asked.

"Oh, yes," I said softly. "The sukiyaki was terrific. Everything was terrific."

"Next week we'll learn about Hawaii," she said. "That is, if I can borrow a grass skirt from someone and can learn to make sweet-and-sour pork by then."

I reached across the table to hold her hand. "I need to tell you something. The past few weeks I've felt like a tiny leaking life raft in the middle of a big ocean during a storm. But then you came along and somehow you renewed me, and now I'm ready to face the storm again. I just want to say thanks."

She threw me a coy Oriental look, silently gave me a homemade fortune cookie. The promise made in it was also homemade and soon fulfilled.

Chapter Fifteen

It was November. Over the past few months we had worked as partners. The business had done well enough that we could afford a little vacation to California, mainly for Adam and me to see Disneyland.

We sat on a park bench overlooking the ocean and watched Adam climb a jungle gym.

It was late afternoon and the sun was floating in oranges and reds on the water. When I checked my wallet to see how our money was holding out, I saw the picture of Charly.

"It moved again," Lara said excitedly.

I reached down and touched her melon-sized tummy. Somebody's knee lightly bumped my hand.

"Terrific," I smiled. "He kicks like a boy."

"She's a ballet dancer," she countered with a smile.

Pulling the picture from my wallet, I gave it to Lara. "Keep this for me, okay?"

She looked at the picture. "She was wonderful for you, wasn't she."

"She was very good for me."

"And you'll always love her more than me, won't you."

I had thought about it before, knowing sometime she'd ask.

"Look at the sunset—isn't it beautiful?"

She shrugged her shoulders. "It's okay if you don't answer. I shouldn't have asked."

"I'm not avoiding the question. Which of all the sunsets you've ever seen do you love the most?"

"The first one?" she answered, anticipating the worst.

"I don't think so. Every time we see a sunset our appreciation is built on the ones we've already experienced. The older I get, the more amazed I am that a miracle like a sunset still exists. And that's the way I feel about my love for you."

Overhead a plane etched its vanishing trail across the sky.

"Lara, I guess it's not surprising I remarried, but what surprises me is how much I love you. It's a miracle you came along."

She snuggled closer to me.

We watched the evening sky until it was dark, then the three of us walked back to our motel room.